SAMANTHA LEIGH is a t[illegible]
a lifetime of consuming contempo[illegible]
pizza when hungover, she graduated from the MA in Writing at LJMU, where she set out to write the book she had always wanted to read. A professional millennial mess, 'Joy' is her first novel, unravelling the chaos of navigating your twenties and the drama that goes along with it.

Follow Samantha on X @SammyWrites_

JOY

SAMANTHA LEIGH

Northodox Press Ltd
Maiden Greve, Malton,
North Yorkshire, YO17 7BE

This edition 2024

1
First published in Great Britain by
Northodox Press Ltd 2024

ISBN: 978-1-915179-33-3

This book is set in Caslon Pro Std

For my Nan, who would have wished that this were a murder mystery novel.

1

2012 / LIVERPOOL

The rain had been especially heavy the first day that Erica met Joy. Her fine art class had just been dismissed, and having achieved nothing of particular merit, she made her way out to the rickety and rusting old bus stop that the college had erected to shove the smokers into.

Opening the back entrance door and staring into the rainy gloom of the car park, she considered retreating, until her body's need for nicotine forced her forwards. The harsh October wind stung Erica's cheeks as she lit up a cigarette. She shielded the flame with her hand and sat on the single blue metal bar that ran along the inside of the shelter. Erica often suspected it to be purposefully uncomfortable, as to dissuade the students from continuing the habit.

She pulled her jacket tighter around herself and dragged on her cigarette. She heard the furious clicking of another lighter followed by an exasperated sigh, as a girl she hadn't seen at college before came bursting out of the door. She took a seat on the bar next to Erica. Her hair was cut into one of those Uma-Therman-in-Pulp-Fiction-style bobs, which thanks to the Liverpool wind was in a state of disarray. The girl threw a Harrington jacket around her shoulders and sighed heavily.

Do you have a lighter?

Yes, Erica said, whilst staring, presumably like a moron as she dug clumsily around in her pocket for her light. She found it, handed it over. Cheap from the off license, it had a neon smiley face printed on it. The girl took it, grazing Erica's fingers with hers as she did so, lit her cigarette, and then tucked the lighter into her own pocket. Erica didn't object.

Words. Words. Words. Erica desperately searched her brain for words, something that might sound cool or aloof, intriguing even, to this girl that she had immediately decided was used to being unimpressed by others. She did not want to be one of those people.

The girl leant her head against the back of the grim shelter, inhaling smoke and blowing it back into the damp air. Her hair stuck to the condensation on the Perspex glass. Erica watched the smoke leave her black painted lips. She rolled her head and met Erica's gaze, a soft smile that made her stomach dance in a way she hadn't felt before. Before Erica could speak again, the girl stubbed her cigarette against the wall of the shelter and dropped it onto the floor before getting to her feet.

Thanks for the light, she said.

Erica just nodded, awestruck, as she watched the girl bounce off back inside the door to the college, back to whichever class she emerged from, the laces of her battered Doc Martens flying wildly behind her, Erica's lighter still in her pocket. She watched as the door closed with a heavy clunk, her heart pounding against the wall of her small chest. She realised that she had dropped her own cigarette onto the floor, its embers being soaked into the murky puddles at her feet. She could feel her pulse in her throat. It was then that Erica realised two things.

One, she needed to see that girl again, and two, a suspicion she had long held about herself had been confirmed, and she felt free.

2

2019 / LONDON

Joy sits on the toilet with the seat down and stares at her phone. If this dinner party doesn't end soon, she might have to invent a dicky tummy or period pain and spend the rest of the evening locked in here. She can hear them cackling through the walls, interrupting her pretend wee.

Joy? A voice comes from behind the door.

Sorry, yep, coming. *Times up.*

She flushes the toilet for plausible effect and washes her hands, stuffs her phone into her back pocket. Why do they only put pockets on the back of women's jeans? What company decided that a rectangular arse was better than a regular one? Clearly a ploy to force all women to buy handbags.

She opens the bathroom door to her husband, Sebastian. He's red wine drunk. She can tell from the lazy smile on his face. The slight purple staining on his bottom lip.

Long time in there, babe.

Needed a dump, sorry.

Eurgh, he recoils as Joy laughs.

It was a joke, Seb, Jesus. She laughs some more.

Disgusting. You can't talk like that tonight, not around them. He gestures to the dining room behind him.

He pushes past her into the bathroom and sits on the toilet. Definitely red wine drunk - sit down wees are a sure sign. At least it stops him pissing on the toilet seat. Who said romance is dead?

You're having fun then? Joy lingers by the door.

Oh, yeah. Jason was just talking about the divorce though, boooring.

He chuckles to himself. Joy doesn't respond, just leaves the bathroom and shuts the door behind her.

Jason is a regular guest in their home, always invited to the monthly Sunday roast that they host. He recently divorced his wife of two years. Joy had always quite liked her; she could put away a lot of Sauvignon Blanc and didn't ask any personal questions. The perfect guest. But no, not anymore. Jason had apparently cheated on her with an expensive dominatrix during a business trip to Paris a few months ago, a fact he seems somewhat proud of. She's taking half of everything. The cars, the townhouse, his trust fund. Joy thinks that he should be less devastated about losing his stuff and more so about now having to convince another poor woman that he isn't total human garbage.

She grabs a fresh bottle of wine from the fridge and heads into the dining room. Yes, a separate dining room. In London. North London. She would be constantly in awe of how lucky she is if she wasn't bored shitless by it. The scene in the dining room is one of content relaxation. Main meals were eaten an hour ago, her homemade panna cotta went down a treat for dessert. Now she just has to present a monstrously big cheeseboard and wait for them to leave. She takes a deep breath and smiles, three faces gleam back at her. She grins back as if she knows more than one of them.

Cracking food, Joy. *Jason, gross, no need to wink as he said that.*

Yes, sweetheart. Well done, madness that you don't use help. *Senior doctor at Seb's surgery, slight racist vibes, big red nose.*

Yes, astonishing really, I could never. *Wife of Big Red Nose. Evident lover of having a plastic surgeon as a husband.*

Seb returns to his seat at the head of the table and they all clink glasses, praising her food. Validation washes over her like a hot shower on a cold morning. She hates herself for craving their approval. They see her as nothing more than Sebastian's wife/chef/cleaner, but what else is she these days, anyway? She gracefully accepts the complements. She places a carefully arranged board of seven different (artisanal, whatever that means) cheeses, grapes, crackers and chutneys in front of them. They disassemble it with care, manners.

Joy thinks of how she used to eat, before she met Seb and he told her how gross it was. Well, he actually used the word *uncouth*, but that's just posh person for *gross*. She would devour her food enthusiastically, with her hands, with noises of satisfaction and enjoyment, with passion. She tries to conjure in her mind the last time she enjoyed anything like that. Her love for food has wilted these last few years, her love for anything. Aside from her dog, that is. Bernie the Golden Retriever was purchased for her by Seb last year as an attempt to plaster over her sadness after he had given up trying to fix it. She had been too sad to function. Slept constantly. Had stopped exercising, instead choosing to throw up after meals to keep her figure. Her old friend Valencia always did it in uni, and she looked amazing. Still does. It wasn't sustainable though. Her Dad had spent too much money on her teeth as a child to have them rot away for the sake of a disease she didn't really have.

Seb hadn't been irritated by her sadness when they first met, she had introduced him to The Smiths and neat whiskey. He thought it was edgy, mysterious, intriguing. During last year's episode, he had told her that it was finally time to grow up, join the real world, that she had nothing to be sad about. He placed an eight-week-old Bernie into her arms, and she forgave him immediately for those words. She suddenly had a reason to enjoy life again.

She hears him bark from the other room. He wants to be with people. Seb doesn't like him roaming free during dinner parties though, says it's rude. Also, he has a fondness for sneaking food off of people's plates.

So, Seb, Jason begins, shame this lass you said you'd set me up with cancelled, I feel like a right fifth wheel.

Joy's ears perk up.

Yeah, she couldn't make it down in the end. I think you two would have hit it off otherwise.

Typical, thought she might be a catfish anyway, or that you were having me on. He chuckles to himself as he sips the last of his wine. He motions for Joy to top off his glass. She does. Always a great hostess.

A set up? Who was that with? She directs the question at Seb, attempting to keep her voice light. Trying hard not to show the irritation she feels about not being consulted in the decision of what unwitting woman they would expose to Jason.

Valencia.

Val? She said she wanted to be set up?

Well, not exactly. But you know, she's always by herself. It's criminal.

Huh. Why's that? Joy leans back in her chair.

Seb looks at her knowingly. It is obvious that he thinks Val's singleness is criminal because she is attractive and a bit famous, but he won't say as much.

Well, she's a good mate isn't she. Don't like to see good mates alone. He slaps Jason on the back in that weird matey way that men do. Displaying affection, but just enough to assure everybody that they are not, in fact, homosexual. Joy resists the urge to point out that Val is alone by choice, and Jason is alone because he likes paying women to have sex with him behind his wife's back.

Plus, her pictures on Instagram are insane, I wouldn't say no, Jason says. The rest of the table laughs.

As if Jason is even worth the train fare from Liverpool.

Joy smiles tightly, takes a large sip of her wine. Seb eyes her, and then the glass. The glare that says, mind yourself, darling, how many is that? She chooses to ignore it, drains the glass. If they fight over it later, at least it will give them something to do.

Bernie barks again from the other room. Joy makes to get up, but is eyed once again by Seb.

He's fine, Joy. You can take him out after dinner, once everybody is finished.

She returns her behind to the seat. Pours herself another glass of wine and loads some cheese onto her plate. She watches as Big Red Nose's wife slides a thin piece of brie onto her plate along with two apple slices. She didn't eat much of the dinner, Joy noticed. Her new-found jaw pain from a recent surgery ensuring discomfort with every bite. Chatter resumes around the table, the three men discussing the recent problems with the new booking system at the surgery that is causing chaos. Joy drowns them out, her focus solely on what this woman is about to do with the brie. Seb said that this most recent procedure is the fourth on her face, rendering her an expressionless husk, remnant of an eighty's movie star, but like, the wax version. The recovery seems to be taking its toll on her aging bone structure, every movement looks an effort.

Joy watches as she cuts a tiny corner off of the cheese with her knife, slides it onto a slice of apple. She brings it to her pouty mouth, puts it down again. Her husband looks over at her and smiles lovingly, puts his hand on hers. Joy wonders if he is aware that his handiwork has robbed his wife of enjoying any food that she has to chew.

Her attention is returned to the table at the mention of her name.

Yes, yes, she's booked in in a few months' time, aren't you babe? Finally making use of the perks of being married to one of us. His laugh echoes throughout the room.

What's she getting done? Jason asks Seb, as if she isn't sitting two feet from him.

Just some lip filler, some Botox in the forehead and cheeks. He looks over at Joy with an expression that could be mistaken for adoration. She knows full well he is picturing how perfect she could be, if she'd just let him work his magic.

Ah, nothing too serious then. You excited? Jason looks at her expectantly.

Oh, erm, yeah, kind of. She laughs awkwardly. Seb knows that she isn't totally sold on the idea yet, but was sick of him pestering.

Careful dear, Big Red Nose's wife pipes up beside her. It's a slippery slope!

They all burst into a collective cackle while Joy's stomach hits the ground three floors below her feet. She feels her hands go clammy. Her mouth is dry. She looks back over at the wife, who is now managing to nibble a corner of the apple slice, the brie abandoned on the plate. She is still giggling through her swollen lips, her Botox cheeks almost creaking with the effort of laughter. That can't be her future.

She suddenly feels trapped in her own body, her breaths coming both far too fast and not at all. She can feel beads of cold sweat forming on her brow, her upper lip. She looks at Seb who smiles back at her, her distress clearly not evident enough on her face for him to notice. Can he not hear her heartbeat? Can none of them? Isn't it deafening them like it is her? She clutches her glass tightly, drains its contents. Tries to place it carefully back on the table but loses her grip, everybody stares as it breaks into two pieces in her hand. A dry gasp of a laugh escapes her mouth, making light of the chaos unfolding inside of her. She picks up both parts of the glass, waving off offers of help from Seb's older co-worker.

It's fine it's fine, I've got it don't worry, who needs another drink?

She darts out of the room, the stem of the glass digging into her palm. Dumps the sparkling remains into the bin and runs cold water over her bloody hand. Fishes out a plaster and slaps it over the tear in her skin. Bernie barks again. He needs to go out. She needs to get out. She grabs her coat from the hallway and releases him from the living room, he bounds excitedly towards her. Shouts to the others that Bernie needs a wee, she will be back in ten. She clips his lead onto his collar. They run down the stairs, out the front door, over the road and into the park opposite. She doesn't breathe out until she gets to a bench and steadies herself.

She unclips Bernie's collar, he runs to chase a nearby pigeon. Her heart tries to swell with love for him, but it is stuck in place, weighed down with the horror of the realisation that her future is written for her, and it looks like that.

Her phone buzzes in her pocket. She expects Seb will be checking on her after such an unusual exit. A shaking hand instead reveals a message from Valencia.

Sorry I didn't make it down tonight, Seb sprung it on me last minute and all the guy posts about on socials is football. No thank yoooou x

She relaxes a little, enjoying the sudden string of communication linking her from this park back to her hometown of Liverpool. Not alone, not alone, not alone.

He didn't even tell me! No wonder, I'd have told you to steer clear. Miss you x

She looks up to check on Bernie, who is busy sniffing the base of a tree. Deep breaths, deep breaths, deep breaths. Calm down, calm down, calm down.

Miss u too babe. Out with Erica and her ball and chain ***eye roll***. I'll say hi from you. Come home soon xo

Joy's stomach flips at the sight of Erica's name. She stares at the screen for a while, trying to envision the scene unfolding two hundred miles north west of her. Val, Erica and her girlfriend, Frankie. All sat around a table in a familiar pub where the staff know their names, drinking together. Joy says hi! She can just see the look on Frankie's face at the mention of her girlfriend's ex. Erica no doubt changing the subject before she can turn it into an argument.

She shakes it off. Life in Liverpool is over for her now. She lives here. With her husband. And her dog. The lucky girl, who married rich, who doesn't need to work. And she's happy. She's in London with her husband and her dog and is happy. Very happy, very happy, very happy.

She pulls a box of cigarettes out of her coat pocket and lights one up. Her hand steadies, the rush of nicotine immediately soothing her busy head. She leans back and looks at the stars, a clear September night. Bernie's soft head finds its way underneath her hand. She is always amazed at a dog's ability to sense anxiety in humans. For the millionth time is thankful that she has him beside her. She ruffles the fur around his ears.

What are we gonna do, buddy? Huh? Do you like it here?

She looks down at her furry companion for answers, but he has none. Just licks her hand and sits at her feet, keeping guard for any rogue wildlife that may need chasing. They sit for a while, enjoying the silence, calming her heart rate. She can't face going back up there. Staring her plastic, stifled, upper middle-class future in the face. This was not the direction she had intended for her life to go in. Her eighteen-year-old self would be so disappointed if she could see her now.

She stubs out her cigarette on top of a nearby bin and clips Bernie's lead back on, gives him a good-boy-treat, which he inhales. They stroll back to the house together, slowing as they approach the building. From the hallway inside, she can hear the raucous drunken laughter of them all. The booming sound of Seb's voice holding court on some obscure aspect of surgical history that only his co-workers would ever find interesting. Their silicon wives expected to smile and nod along, like the dolls they so wish to be. She tries to shake off a vision of herself thirty years from now, permanent stick up her arse, surgically frozen face, laughing at the banal quips of a bunch of posh old men. Pushes the image to the back of her mind as she roots in her pocket for the front door key.

She slips into the house as quietly as possible, trying to lead Bernie into the bedroom without the sound of his paws attracting attention. They make it, and he happily hops onto the bed beside her. She just can't go back in there yet. Not that they've noticed her absence. She wraps herself in the giant woven blanket that decorates a pointless chair in the corner of the bedroom. It's very comfortable, why is this just for decoration? She gets out her phone. Stares at it. Considers texting Erica. Desperately wants to. To call her maybe, to hear her voice, to make her laugh, to feel like she's home. Tries to envisage a scenario in which that action doesn't end in drama. Can't think of one. Tears come, and she doesn't try to fight them. Just wraps the blanket around herself tighter and sobs as quietly as she can, mourning the loss of a life she never had, and the future that she feels she cannot avoid. Bernie places his head on her lap, she holds one of his soft ears between her fingers. Wipes her eyes, eyeliner was a mistake today. To be fair, she wasn't to know that dinner would lead to an existential crisis.

She takes a deep breath, decides to message Seb instead of showing her face back in the dining room.

Reaaallllllyyyyy bad period pain!! Have gone to bed. Say sorry for me, love u x

The two blue ticks appear immediately, and then he goes offline. No response. She supposes that that's better than questions, or a demand for her return to the table, for the sake of politeness.

She grabs the TV remote, gets under the covers and pulls Bernie closer to her. Tomorrow will be better. It has to be.

3

2012 / LIVERPOOL

Three days after Erica met Joy, a large group of students from their art college made their way to the house of a guy who claimed his paintings of orange canvas' were a statement about society. He never expanded further. He consistently got the highest marks in their fine art class. His parents were notoriously liberal, allowing him to host parties for most major holidays whilst they retreated to a hotel in the city together.

Halloween had always been a favourite of Erica's. She loved the chance to dress up ridiculously, make her face up to whatever dramatic expanse she could dream up. House parties also meant that she had a chance to get drunk on cheap alcohol with her friends, without shivering in the cold on the local park. A few months stood between Erica and the legal drinking age. They were dragging.

She and two of her friends from college had spent the whole afternoon getting ready for the party. They painted each-other's faces, sewed costumes together. A thin layer of glittery body paint coated Erica's bedroom floor. As they sipped sickly blue alcopops and put the finishing touches to their costumes, she had considered telling the girls about her encounter in the smoking shelter earlier that week. Wondered if by saying it out loud, her realisation about her sexuality would seem ridiculous, hilarious, something they would refer to in private jokes for years. Or if the words might reverberate within her body and echo throughout the room, their weight and truth undeniable. She said nothing.

The threesome turned up at the party at eight thirty sharp, having caught the Mersey Rail from town all the way out to Formby. Erica slammed the lion shaped knocker in front of them with three heavy throws into the front door. She blew the plastic strands of hair from her wig out of her mouth as she did so. Her friends giggled beside her, pre drinks coursing through their seventeen-year-old veins, the buzz of excitement palpable. The door was opened by Orange Canvas Guy. His attention immediately stolen by the girl to Erica's left, Emma. She had decided on the classic girl-on-Halloween-costume, a cat. Her new push up bra doing all the small talk for her. Confidence poured out of her in a way that Erica had never really grasped. She wondered what it must have been like to be undeniably beautiful.

Orange Canvas Guy gestured for the girls to come inside, his eyes never leaving what Erica hoped was Emma's face, but what she was confident was her chest. It was only as they stepped inside the house that they realised it was not, in fact, a costume party.

Emma shrugged, ever the lover of eyes on herself. She sauntered into the crowd of amused and tipsy teenagers to fetch herself a drink, the host trailing closely behind her, hand on the small of her back. Erica shivered, why did guys do that? A signal to the other guys at the party that this one was his.

Lucy, the other side of Erica, piped up. I'm going home, she said. She reached out for the door handle, but Erica planted herself firmly in front of it. No, you're not abandoning me here to look ridiculous all by myself. Lucy stomped her feet.

Erica, I can't handle stares, you know I can't handle stares, I'm wearing a fucking banana costume, there is peeeeeel on my face.

Erica couldn't help but snort out a little laugh at the elongated description of her elaborate makeup. It had taken ages to do.

Lucy gently shoved Erica out of the way and made her escape down the street, pulling the peel off of her face as she went.

What a waste of bananas, Erica thought. She hoped her Mum wouldn't notice their absence from the fruit bowl in the morning. She watched the human sized yellow figure wobble out of sight at the bottom of the road. Gathered herself. She might be here, Erica thought. She can't leave without looking. Her curiosity about herself, and her overnight infatuation with the smoking shelter girl pushed her forwards into the throng of students. They wore regular clothing, lots of black, a few band t-shirts caught her eye. She shimmied past them into the kitchen, dressed as Ziggy Stardust era David Bowie.

Erica reached the island in the kitchen, which boasted a giant bowl of mystery red liquid claiming to be punch. She thought that that only existed in American teen movies. Apparently not. Sat next to the tepid bowl of fluorescent vomit-waiting-to-happen, were three crates of fancy beers. She cracked the lid on one, marvelling at the fact that he hadn't just bought Asda's own for the party. She had never been friends with a wealthy person before, but as she sipped the sweet beer from the can, she could see the perks. No burning on the way down, no acidic burp immediately after the first gulp. She grabbed another beer and stuffed it into her bag as she made her way out into the garden for a smoke. Had no intention of socialising with anybody else here. Nodded and smiled and laughed quietly along with the people making jokes about her as she walked past them. She spotted Emma on the patio, a cup of the red juice in her hand, sat on Canvas Guy's lap.

Erica walked further into the endless garden, the breeze from the nearby beach wrapping itself around her. She was thankful for the polyester jumpsuit at that point, even if it was covered in sequins. Small groups of people she recognised from college sat in clusters together. Some were passing around a joint, another was focused on one crying girl, the others cooing over her. She could hear the unmistakable sound of somebody being sick nearby. Definitely the fault of the red mystery drink.

The space at the back of his house shocked her. This garden, with its green grass, carefully tended bushes, and decades old trees were miles away from her concrete yard in Aigburth. Somebody had taken the care of stringing fairy lights between the trees that lined the side of the garden. Erica wondered if that was for the party, or if Canvas Guy's parents were the sort of people who enjoyed their garden looking like an enchanted forest. She hoped for the latter, the thought made her smile, and although she had only been out for two hours, she couldn't wait to go home.

The lights illuminated the sequins on Erica's jumpsuit, the disco ball of the garden. She dug around in her bag for a lighter, cursing as she realised that she must have forgotten it, or maybe Lucy nicked it. That thieving banana. The thought of trudging back up the garden and having to make conversation with a stranger for a lighter made her stomach turn, social interactions never had been her strong point. She realised the ridiculousness of this contradiction between her anxious personality and the fact that she was standing in a near stranger's garden, alone, with a bright red wig on.

She emptied the contents of her bag out onto the grass, half hoping that a lighter would just materialise in front of her. It did not. She put the cigarette between her front teeth as she shoved her belongings back into the bag, swearing at herself under her breath.

Need a light? A voice in the dark.

As if by magic, there she was. Smoking Shelter Girl stood up from her seat on the root of a huge tree. Oak? She had never paid much attention to foliage. A small flame lit up the space between them, Erica dipped the tip of her cigarette into it, dragging contentedly on it. She caught a glimpse of the lighter, the neon smiley face printed on it staring up at her. Butterflies.

Nice jumpsuit, she said, I love your early work. She winked a glistening brown eye at Erica and smiled a dimpled grin. She gestured for Erica to come and sit under the tree with her. After a large swig of the fancy beer, she did. Words finally came.

I'm Erica, we met the other day? She said it as a question, although she was almost completely certain that she hadn't fabricated the encounter in her head.

I remember, the girl replied. The fairy lights above made her eyes look like they contained entire galaxies. Erica almost forgot how to breathe.

I'm Joy, she said, I was hoping I'd see you again.

Something akin to relief and pure excitement shot through Erica's body. The evening suddenly had so much potential. The noise from the rest of the garden melted away. They clinked their beer cans together, hands lightly brushing as Joy smiled, exhaling smoke into the cold night air.

4

2019 / LIVERPOOL

Erica sits in one of her favourite haunts and holds a delicate wine glass in her hand. She draws a smiley face with her finger on the condensation on the side of it, before taking a sip of its contents. The friendly waiter appears at the table and tops it up with Sauvignon Blanc for her.

The Buyers Club is a hidden gem, tucked away off of Hardman Street. Most might walk straight past it. It is frequented by locals, and in-the-know students, a sanctuary for those wanting to avoid the usual scenes of hungover stag dos and hen parties in the city centre on a Sunday.

She leans back and takes another sip of her wine, happy in the knowledge that a roast dinner is being prepared in the kitchen and will soon be in front of her. Her favourite meal of the week, and given that she has no culinary talent whatsoever, this place suits her down to the ground.

Erica looks across to her girlfriend of one year, Frankie. A blonde bombshell that she met on a horrendous night out in town, she is five years Erica's junior. That wouldn't normally sound like a lot, Erica thinks, but they are wildly different.

Frankie takes a selfie on snapchat with the 'soft glow' filter and posts it to Instagram and Facebook, caption #BestLunchEver. She shows Erica, who smiles.

Babe, we haven't eaten it yet, it might be shit, you don't want to be outed as a liar on the internet.

Frankie looks at her phone screen, genuinely concerned for a moment, before realising that Erica is joking.

That's not *funny*, she says, kicking Erica gently under the table. Some of my followers actually *care* where I am, and I don't want to send them somewhere bad.

Erica takes another drink, wondering how to arrange her words in a way that won't upset her girlfriend.

Sweetie, you have like, five hundred followers. I'm not sure that's quite *influencer* territory.

The look in Frankie's eyes makes her want to eat her words and pretend they never came out of her mouth. She constantly forgets how sensitive her girlfriend is.

I'm trying, Frankie says in a small voice.

I know, babe, I'm sorry. Erica reaches over and pulls Frankie's hand off of her phone, squeezes it. Want a cocktail? That'll cheer you up I bet.

Sure, she says, grabbing the menu and selecting the one that claims to have 'extra sparkle'. Erica suspects that she may be paying an extra five quid for a sparkler in the glass.

Val should be here soon, Erica says, checking to see if she has any texts from her.

Ohhh, I'm nervous.

Come on, Franks. You've met her a bunch of times, she's just a person.

Babe, she's *famous*. Like, she's a *big* deal.

On Instagram.

Yeah, exactly.

Erica thinks that she must have been absent the day that they were all taught the value of online fame. Val's career is a constant source of mystery to her. People send her clothes, jewellery, food, drinks, umbrellas, sunglasses, vibrators probably, you name it, for her to sample, judge, and advertise to her two million followers. She keeps up the front that she is a staunch vegan, deluding people into believing that she doesn't smash McDonald's cheeseburgers into her face after every night out. Frankie wants nothing more than to do that as a job. She currently works at a makeup counter in Debenhams. They put her up front straight away, her aesthetic reeling in both women looking for know-how and advice, and men who buy things from her in the hopes she might shag them, not realising that she isn't straight.

Erica had barely used her social media accounts when she met Frankie, other than for posting the occasional picture to update her family and old friends of what she looks like now. That soon changed. Frankie gave her a tutorial of all the social apps, showed her how to post her artwork on Instagram, which, to be fair, has gotten her more customers. It just didn't matter that much to Erica when she was younger, she was busy doing real life.

She wonders if she and Frankie are so different that one day, they might run out of stuff to talk about. As she is about to make the mistake of verbalising that thought, Valencia appears at the door of the restaurant. Glamorous as always, the afternoon light shines in behind her making her appear saintly, here to bestow blessings upon any lucky enough to be in her presence. Frankie immediately sits up straight, like an eager pupil desperate to impress the teacher. Val kisses them both on their cheeks and takes a seat next to Frankie, who looks beside herself with happiness at this development.

So good to see you both, Val says, I'm absolutely famished. She beckons the waiter over and orders a double gin and tonic, shimmies out of her faux fur coat and relaxes into her chair.

Busy day? Erica asks.

Like you wouldn't believe. I got sent a whole box of new KvD Makeup to advertise so my face is like, red raw from doing seven looks in one morning, and some twat photoshopped a picture of my face onto somebody at Fazenda, so people are kicking off at me.

Why would people care that you were at Fazenda?

The meat place, Erica. I'm vegan, remember? I got at least

eleven death threats; it wasn't even a good photoshop job. People are insane.

What the fuck? Erica says.

I know, crazy.

The waiter brings Val's drink, and she drains half of it in three sips. Let's out a big sigh of relief.

Christ, I needed that. I've had to just turn my phone off and wait for it to go away.

Frankie looks at her, her expression one of morbid curiosity, clearly trying to resist the urge to check Val's Instagram and see what everyone is saying.

I could never turn my phone off, Frankie says, it's literally like, glued to me, isn't it babe?

It is, yeah.

Val meets Erica's eye, knowing full well how frustrating her friend finds this trait in her partner.

Did you order food for me? Val asks, as three steaming plates appear at their table.

Yeah, don't worry, got you the vegan one, Erica says with a wink.

They thank the waiter; Frankie picks up her phone and snaps a few pictures of her food.

What's a good caption, do you think?

She directs the question at Erica, who is already too lost in roast potatoes to care.

If you post that, Val says, would you mind not tagging me in it? I'd rather people not know where I am for a few days if that's okay.

Frankie's face falls. Her friends are apparently all so jealous that she knows Valencia, and if she can't post it on her story, she won't get any legit bragging points.

Oh, yeah sure, I completely understand. She puts her phone down dejectedly and picks at her food. She watches as Val piles her food high on her fork, making her way around the plate efficiently and enthusiastically. Usually nobody beats Erica for speed eating, but Val does today.

Oh, my, *God,* Val says, that was insane. She leans back in her chair and pats her stomach, washes it down with the rest of her drink.

Frankie eats her vegetables and half of the Yorkshire pudding, avoids the fat attached to the beef.

Erica makes an elongated mmmmm sound, mops up the last of her gravy with a bit of Yorkshire pudding.

That was so good, it's literally never disappointing here, she says.

Val and Frankie nod in agreement.

You not hungry, Franks? Erica asks, seeing her half full plate.

I just don't want to be bloated for drinks after, that's all.

We're going for drinks? Val asks.

Sounds like you need a few.

Hell yeah, I do. Wanna get another round first? I'm just going to nip to the loo, order me another gin?

She saunters to the bathroom, the gazes of at least four men fixed firmly on her.

Erica piles the plates up for the waiter and orders more drinks when he collects them, watches Frankie touch up her lipstick in her compact mirror. Erica surveys her own reflection in the mirrored plant pot in front of her. Freckled face, heavy eyeliner, wild orange mane. Same as always. Frankie pulls a mini hairbrush out of her purse and combs it through her thick hair, pouting into the small mirror.

The affection she feels towards her girlfriend is tinged with something else, but she can't put her finger on it. Val returns to the table as the drinks do.

It's good to have you out, Erica says as they clink their glasses together.

Eurgh, well, I wasn't going to be, I was almost in London, Val explains, tucking her thick dark hair behind her ears. Joy and Seb are having some dinner with his work people, he tried to set me up with this creep he's friends with. I almost went too, praise the lord for being able to stalk people on social media, otherwise I might have been murdered and turned into a lamp or something.

That bad? Erica laughed.

That bad, I've no idea how Joy deals with his lurky pals.

From the corner of her eye, Erica sees Frankie prickle at the mention of Joy's name.

I should really text her actually, Val says, she's stuck all alone at this god-awful dinner with plastic surgeons and their weird robot wives.

Val fishes her phone out of her bag and switches it on, ignores her mountain of notifications and texts Joy.

Sorry I didn't make it down tonight, Seb sprung it on me last minute and all the guy posts about on socials is football. No thank yoooou x

She puts the phone down on the table. Notifications from different apps light up the screen like a Christmas tree having a seizure. Frankie does a terrible job of pretending not to stare at it. A minute later, Joy's reply comes.

He didn't even tell me! No wonder, I'd have told you to steer clear. Miss you x

Is she okay? Erica asks casually, she hopes. Frankie looks at her, but she intentionally doesn't look back.

Apparently Seb didn't even tell her he'd invited me, typical. She says I was right for avoiding, I'll tell her you both say hi, then this thing is getting turned off again.

She finishes typing and throws her phone back into her bag.

So, Val says with a smile, shall we get plastered?

5

2013 / LIVERPOOL

They had both been in tears all morning, neither of them able to believe that the day was finally here. Joy was leaving for university in Brighton. Her dream course was taking her to the opposite end of the country. Erica, a year younger, was set to meet her down there in exactly twelve months, her grades on track to get her into the same university. They planned to rent a small bohemian flat together, spend weekends in the vintage stores, drinking cans of gin and tonic on the pebbled beach, pushing pennies into slot machines at the arcades. It was going to be perfect.

It's one year, just one year, Joy repeated for the millionth time as she held Erica's red and puffy face in her hands. Tears soaked her sleeves, succumbing to her own every time Erica managed to get hers under control. It had almost been a year since they got together on Halloween, inseparable ever since. They had spent their last night together sitting on the roof of Erica's mum's garage, listening to music, drinking cheap wine. Many evenings had been spent this way, preferring each-others company over anything else.

Joy rubbed at her wrist; Erica told her not to. That it would be healed in a few days. The previous night, after too many drinks, tattooing each other had seemed like a great idea. I'm going to be a professional somebody, Erica had said as she dipped a needle into ink she got off of eBay. Joy lifted up the sleeve of her hoody, the crude and slightly shaky outline of a seagull soaring. A reminder of where you come from, Erica had said. Joy had attempted to tattoo the same shape onto Erica's ankle, but chickened out before the needle hit her skin.

Next time I see you, you'd better bloody have one for me, Joy laughed.

I will! I promise.

Erica's mum, Ida, brought in two plates of beans on toast, insisted that they ate all of it, said she had heard what time they stumbled to bed and noticed her vodka had disappeared. Ida ruffled the hair on Erica's head, turning her auburn pixie cut into a spiky mess. Erica flung a bean at her; Ida caught it and threw it back. Joy would miss moments like these.

She was constantly in awe of how cool Erica's parents were. If she had dared to touch her dad's vodka, there'd have been hell to pay. Not that he ever left alcohol lying around. No bottle would ever be left alone long enough to gather dust in her house.

Kevin will be ready to leave in twenty, okay? You sure you don't want to swing by your dad's and say goodbye, my love?

The concern that Ida had for Joy's home life was touching.

I'm sure, I said goodbye when I collected my stuff the other day, she lied. She nodded in the direction of her belongings, stuffed into suitcases and bin bags.

Well, if you're sure.

Ida smiled at them both and left them to eat their breakfasts together. The gratitude that Joy had for Ida and Kevin made her heart swell. They had essentially taken her in when her dad's drinking got out of hand. Kevin was even driving her down to Brighton so that she didn't have to get the train with all her stuff. Her own dad had promised to be sober enough to take her himself, but when she collected the last of her things from home it was clear that that wasn't going to happen. He and his girlfriend were slowly hot boxing the living room with sickly sweet smoke, barely able to maintain eye contact. He had asked Erica to go to the offy before she left, he needed more lager. She refused. His girlfriend went instead, he was happy to let her drive like that. She understood why her Mum left so long ago. Wouldn't miss that place.

It was time for them to set off, 9 a.m. sharp. Kevin finished loading her suitcases and bags into the car and declared that they should hit the motorway now that rush hour had ended. Erica's stomach was full of rocks. She and Joy held each other tightly.

This is so silly, Joy said. You're visiting in a few weeks; we're being so dramatic. The pair laughed at themselves, wiped each-others tears away.

You're right, Erica said. Trains are booked, you'd better find the cheapest and grossest bars as soon as you can, so you know where to take me. She lifted Joy's chin with her hand and kissed her. Electricity every time.

I love you.

I love you too.

Erica watched her dad's car pull off the kerb, Joy waved at her out of the window until she was out of sight. She was so proud of her in that moment, so excited for their future, even if it meant some pain right now.

Not long, pet, not long. Ida pulled Erica close to her and let the last of her hot tears soak into her blouse.

Come on, my love, let's go for a nice walk, eh? Beautiful day for it. I'll get us an ice cream on Sefton Park.

It's like nine o'clock?

Such things don't matter when the heart is hurting. She pulled her daughter in closer. Go get wrapped up, it's bloody freezing.

Erica did as she was told. Pulled herself together. At least it was Sunday, her absolute favourite. We've got this, she thought. We've got this.

6

2019 / LONDON

The call comes at four thirty a.m. on the twenty-sixth of September, four nights after their dinner party. Possibly the only people left in the country besides the elderly that have a house phone, its shrill cry alerts Bernie from his slumber at once, his resounding barks forcing his humans out of the bliss of their unconscious states.

It is almost never good news, getting a phone call at that time. With births being the exception, there is no good news that can't wait until sociable hours. Joy opens her eyes and lets them adjust to the darkness. She hasn't dreamt it; the phone is still ringing. Seb is doing a terrible job of pretending to sleep through it. Bernie bounces into the room and jumps straight on the bed. The resulting noise from Seb means that he has landed on a sensitive area.

Fucking dog, fucking phone. Who's ringing the sodding house phone at this time?

Joy doesn't respond, just calls Bernie onto the floor next to her and settles him down. She hears Seb pick up the phone. Who even has their house number? Who would choose to use it instead of a mobile? Surely it can't be cold callers at this time in the morning. Joy pictures a man in a call centre on the other side of the world, accidentally pushing the seven instead of the eight and trying to sell diet products to an unwitting sleepy brit at four a.m.

She can hear Seb murmur responses into the handset, and

then the unmistakable trill as he slams the receiver down. She hopes he hasn't damaged it. She found that weird old phone at a market in Camden a few years ago. Bright red and ghastly, she had to have it.

It's my Mum, Seb says in a strained voice as he comes back into the room. He pulls down luggage from on top of the wardrobes, starts shoving random t shirts into it.

What? Is she okay? Joy sits up in bed.

They don't know, she's in hospital, that was her doctor, she must have written down our landline as her emergency contact.

What's happened to her? Joy watches as he stuffs some of her summer clothes and a pair of his old swim trunks into the suitcase.

She fell, apparently. I always fucking tell her to move somewhere without stairs, and does she listen? No. And now look what's happened. He throws one of her Iggy Pop shirts onto the floor in exasperation and falls down onto the bed.

Hey, hey, it's gonna be okay. She strokes his head, a technique that roused him from many hungover 'I want to die' holes over the years. Take a breath, what do we need to do?

Well, I need go to there don't I? Liverpool, now.

Joy's stomach flips. He wants to go alone? She thinks of him back in their home city, and feels an immediate pang of jealousy.

I could come with you? It's not like I'm doing anything here.

No, no. That's not fair. Stay here, have the place to yourself.

Joy's eyes narrow. *Why does he want to go alone?*

It's fine, really. Unless there's like, a *reason* you want to go alone, then sure…

Oh, don't be so paranoid, Joy. My Mum is in hospital, and you're worried about me shagging about?

I didn't say that, you did.

He throws his hands up in exasperation.

Fine. Come. If it'll make you feel better, come.

She nods. Realises that she has just gotten herself into looking after her broken mother-in-law. *Shit.* They haven't visited home in so long. The thought makes her nauseous and indescribably happy at the same time. Her mouth is dry.

Seb takes a deep breath.

If we leave in half an hour, we can be there by the time visiting hours open up.

Right. Joy nodded along to this information. Right, yes, of course.

She surveys the state of the suitcase in front of them.

Okay. You go and make coffees, I'll pack.

He does as he is told and leaves the room, tapping away on the screen of his phone. Joy flicks the main light on and rubs her eyes. Removes everything he stuffed into the suitcase out again. What will they need?

SEB? She shouts.

WHAT? He shouts back from the kitchen. If the neighbours get pissed off, at least they won't be here to deal with it for a few days.

HOW MANY DAYS ARE WE GOING FOR?

His head appears in the doorway.

Stop shouting, it's late. Or is it early? Fuck. Erm, I don't know? A few weeks, I guess?

He double takes at Joy's expression.

What? Problem? He tilts his head in mock confusion. I told you, I can go alone if you like.

N-no. All good. I just wasn't expecting it to be that long a visit, that's all.

No, yeah, you're totally right. Let's just leave my broken mother to fend for herself, shall we? Christ, Joy.

Sorry. I didn't mean it like that. I just meant like, for packing purposes.

Good.

She folds up shirts and jeans, rolls up a couple of scarves, remembering how chilly the autumn months could be up north. She pulls another suitcase down from the wardrobe, starts shoving pairs of shoes for different occasions into it. You never know, she thinks, there might be time to socialise. She could see Valencia, even. The thought brightens her mood immediately. Yes, they could meet for cocktails and maybe see a film. And if Erica is there, well... she wouldn't be opposed to seeing her, either. A voice inside of her tells her that that is the only reason she wants to go. She bats it away, that's nonsense. She is going so that she can be a supportive, loving wife. A good daughter-in-law. Yep. She throws a few of her favourite black dresses in there for good measure, you never know when the occasion for a nice dress might occur, right?

Seb returns to the bedroom with two cups of coffee.

Did you make mine with almond milk?

He huffs and leaves the room again. All these years of being together and he still forgets that she can't stand cow's milk. Probably most men forget these small details about their wives.

Thirty-two minutes later, Joy is locking up the door as Seb pulls the Range Rover up to the front of the house. The sky is still dark, Joy's breath visible in the crisp air. Bernie looks up at her as they load up the car with suitcases, confused as to what all the fuss is about. She coaxes him into the boot of the car and piles up some biscuits in front of him, kisses his nose before she shuts the door. Seb sets the Sat Nav for Formby. Barely even Liverpool, in Joy's opinion. His Mum's house looks more like a manor in the middle of the Lake District than a house that's a twenty-minute drive from Bootle.

Joy considers texting Val to let her know about her imminent arrival, but decides against it. She wants it to be a surprise. It will add a little purpose to her visit, aside from being verbally abused by her injured mother-in-law.

The Sat Nav announces that they will arrive at their destination in four hours and fifteen minutes.

The countdown begins.

7

2013 / BRIGHTON

Erica arrived at Brighton station after three train journeys that had been full of stress and delays. She had never been to London before, let alone caught connecting trains through it, and the sheer pace of everybody in Euston was enough to bring her to a panicked halt. She had navigated, slowly, to the annoyance of locals, through the tube station at Euston to Victoria. She clung to her bag, the speech about thieves that Ida had given her that morning echoing in her head. A man had stared at her unashamedly from across the carriage as they swayed with the motion of the train, his gaze aimed at her chest, hand in his pocket. At the announcement of her stop, she had all but legged it off. But she had made it, finally. She stood at the entrance to the train station, her eyes searching for Joy's face in the busy Friday crowd. Erica had never seen such an eclectic mix of people in one place. From her vantage point, she could see a group of 'lads lads lads' outside of the train station pub, a hoard of hen parties dressed in sparkles and laughter, wrangling a cheap looking veil into the updo of a cackling tanned blonde woman. Rolling cigarettes at the entrance were groups of hippies in bright, baggy clothing with dreadlocks. She could see a pair of trad goths outside of the Tesco sharing a bag of chips, both clad in black, hair backcombed within an inch of its life.

So many subcultures existing in one place, and nobody seemed to be batting an eyelid. She thought it odd, but liked it. She could see the appeal of this place, and hadn't even really set foot in it yet. Already her excitement to start Uni here next year was growing. She looked up at the seagulls swarming overhead. A glimpse of familiarity above.

She heard her name being called and spotted Joy immediately, confidently striding towards her. She wore her trademark black skinny jeans, a Smiths shirt tucked into them, battered Doc Martens on her feet. Her face sparkled with new jewellery, her nose ring now connected to her earring with some sort of delicate chain, her slick black hair immaculate as always, even in the wind.

Erica wanted to run to her, but was rooted to the spot. Joy reached her, they flung their arms around each other, hugged tightly. She held Erica's shoulders and looked at her face as if she hadn't seen it in years. She planted a kiss on Erica's lips, then five more. How had they gone this long without hugging? Without kissing? How was either one of them still standing after being apart for this long?

They linked hands and walked away from the station, all the words they hadn't spoken to each other the last four weeks spilling out into the space between them.

We'll go to my favourite pub, Joy said, my friend Valencia from halls is meeting us there, you're going to love her. Some people from my course really want to meet you, too.

Erica's stomach dropped a little. She wasn't great with strangers, even less so with ones that already had such a strong connection with her girlfriend.

Sounds great, she said.

We'll get some lunch too; you must be bloody starving.

Erica nodded. She had a sandwich and snacks for the whole journey, but managed to get through them all on the first train down to London. An appetite like no other.

After a bunch of twists and turns through colourful lanes and busy streets, they arrived at the pub. As they entered, a table full of people greeted Joy.

Erica, she said, these are my friends from my course.

She grinned as she introduced everybody, the names fell out of Erica's head just as quickly as they had entered. Her shoulder ached from the bag hanging on it, her face grew hot under inspection from the people at the table.

Sit, sit, I'll get us drinks. Joy manhandled her onto a wooden stool and sauntered off to the bar. Six sets of expectant eyes looked at her.

So, said a girl with bright pink dreadlocks, you're the famous girlfriend?

Oh, I don't know about famous, haha. Erica picked at the skin around her fingers under the table.

Famous in our conversations, alright. Joy's always banging on about you, Pink Dread girls continued.

Yeah, I mean, she hasn't said much about you to me, but that's because we only get like, four classes a week together. This came from the girl sat directly across from Erica, dressed in paint splattered overalls and drinking a red wine. Erica noticed old lipstick stains on the side of the glass.

So, Erica, tell us, what sort of art do you make?

Erica gazed around the table at the array of outfits and hairstyles, realising she'd never referred to herself as an artist. Joy must have told them that Erica was coming to study here too.

I like illustration and painting; I'd love to do something cool like be a tattoo artist.

The people around the table exchanged glances. Was that a bad thing here?

Oh, Overalls Girl said. We just assumed, you know, because of the conceptual sort of art that Joy makes, you'd be the same. I, for example, am interested in the decay of the human body, and how decay really begins at birth. She sipped her red wine, visibly tried not to wince at it.

Yes, and my work is focused on the form of the female body, and how the label of 'beauty' changes depending on the perspective, Pink Dreads girl said, satisfied with this summary of her work.

Mine, the mousey guy with huge glasses in the corner said, is usually centred around death, most of my work is expressive mark making and performance pieces in which I push myself to different physical and emotional boundaries.

Wow, Erica said, that's all… so interesting. She silently thanked the heavens when Joy returned with a drink in each hand, bag of crisps hanging in her mouth.

What did I miss? She asked.

Just catching your wifey up on what we all do. You didn't tell us she wants to be a tattoo artist, how cute.

Joy missed the note of sarcasm in Large Glasses' voice.

She's going to be great, she said, revealing the shaky lines slightly resembling a seagull on her wrist, healed now, and squeezed Erica's hand encouragingly.

Her friends around the table all nodded in fake enthusiasm, one of them looked like Joy had just shown her a decapitated rat in the street.

Erica took a large sip of her drink. This isn't what she thought they would be doing on the first day of their reunion. She wanted to go and see Joy's halls, wanted to tear into her like she hadn't been able to do for the few weeks. Joy smiled at her in between conversations with her friends. She tried to involve Erica in all of them, but to no avail. She had shrunk into herself, intimidated by every single one of these self-assured assholes.

The mood shifted with the arrival of a beautiful woman at the bar. Erica recognised her from pictures that Joy had posted recently. The gang beckoned her over, Joy introduced her as Valencia, Val for short. She plonked herself down next to Erica and proceeded to fawn over her customised thrifted jacket. Erica had dedicated months to stitching different band patches and badges onto it, she wore it everywhere. Val asked her about almost every single patch, compared bands that they both listened to, swore she would listen to the ones she hadn't already. Seeing this, the others turned their attention to Erica, too. Suddenly enamoured with her presence, in awe of her homemade jacket, interested in her career plans.

Val saw the discomfort in her and offered her a cigarette. Erica took it gladly. Joy said she'd be out in a moment, that she needed the loo. The pair of them stood out the back of the pub and lit up.

Ignore them, Val said on an exhale, absolute twats.

Erica laughed and coughed on the smoke.

It's nice to hear you say that.

Joy appeared in the doorway, cigarette between her teeth.

Having fun, babe? She looked expectantly at Erica.

Oh yeah, everybody's really… nice.

Aren't they?! And so interesting. I swear I thought I was a good artist when I got here, but they have me questioning so much. The course is way more conceptual than I thought.

Erica nodded and dragged on her cigarette.

So, what do you lovebirds have planned this weekend?

Well, we should probably go and drop your stuff off at home.

Erica was slightly taken aback at Joy's use of the word 'home' in relation to her uni halls. This wasn't home. Not yet, surely.

And then, Joy continued, these guys have just invited me to this cool free exhibit down the road, we could go check that out with them? Then they're going for dinner at this new Fairtrade Indian street food place, so we could tag along to that too.

Joy's face shone with excitement, clearly over the moon that she had been accepted by her peers. With every word Joy spoke, Erica's heart dropped a little more. This weekend was supposed to be romantic, with them doing what they did best; being alone together. Erica had envisioned fish and chip lunches on the windy beach, cheap drinks in sticky bars and shared bottles of wine in Joy's bedroom. They had never needed much entertainment outside of each other.

Erica mustered some excitement from within herself. She understood that this was Joy's life now, and in a year, it would be hers too. Val looked between the two of them, reading the situation.

Well, I'd love to stay but I have a date.

Ooh, who is it this time? Joy stubbed her cigarette out on her boot as she spoke.

Just some guy from my course. Turns out not all male fashion students are gay.

Erica laughed at Val's joke.

Wow, said Overalls Girl, who appeared in the doorway with a hand rolled cigarette in her mouth, that's a really fucking offensive stereotype, Valencia.

Joy nodded.

Yes, I know, it was a joke.

Weird thing to joke about, she muttered as she pulled a lighter out of her pocket.

Val kept her pearly smile stretched on her face and announced her departure. She kissed Joy and Erica on their cheeks and pushed past Overalls Girl.

Lovely to meet you, Erica, I'll see you both at home.

Home, there it was again. So weird.

The rest of their table could be heard inside saying goodbye to Val, Overalls Girl seemingly the only one that wasn't in awe of her.

God, she's full of herself, Overalls Girl said.

Erica waited for Joy to defend her friend, the one she met on her first day here. She was looking at her boots. No words came.

I really like her, Erica chimed in on her behalf.

Overalls Girl let a puff of smoke out of her nose and looked Erica up and down, as if to say, of course you do.

Another drink, babe? Joy asked Erica.

Sure, I'm starving too, can we go for lunch somewhere, maybe?

Let's have another drink with these guys first, yeah? Then we'll go drop your stuff off and go from there.

Joy took Erica's hand and led her back inside, past Overalls Girl who refused to budge from the doorway, enjoying being an obstruction. She gestured for her to sit back down at the table and headed to the bar again, but Erica followed her instead.

Babe, Erica said, can we just go back to yours? I kind of just wanna spend time with you, you know?

Oh, but everyone is here to meet you, she nodded in the direction of their table, her friends talking animatedly over each other.

I know, but I'm pretty tired and haven't seen you in like, a month. Can we just go back and chill out and then see them later on? Seems like we're gonna be seeing enough of them this weekend anyway.

Joy looked taken aback.

What does that mean?

Nothing. Just that, I was only really bothered about seeing you this weekend, like we normally do.

Erica, babe, I've made friends here. I've got more of a life here after a month than I had in nineteen years of living in Liverpool. Don't make me feel bad for having friends and wanting them to like you.

Erica supressed the urge to point out that it should be her liking them that Joy should be worried about, not the other way around. Since when was she this much of a people pleaser? In the time that they had known each other, Erica had never known her to be eager for people's friendship. It didn't suit her.

Joy kissed Erica and turned to the barman to order their drinks. That conversation was over then, Erica supposed. She returned to her stool begrudgingly, laughed meekly along to the pretentious jokes and anecdotes about gap years being told around the table. Her stomach rumbled, she hoped there would be a chance for food soon, Joy knew how grumpy she got when she hadn't eaten.

Joy returned to the table and set their drinks down, instantly jumping into their conversation about Blonde Girl in Corner's new piece. She showed them a picture on her phone. A square canvas painted in three different shades of purple.

It represents different class structures in society, Blonde Girl said in earnest.

Erica smiled, waited for Joy to tear into it like they so often did to Orange Canvas Guy in college.

Profound, Pink Hair Girl said.

Yes, and rather provocative, said Big Glasses Guy.

I agree, incredibly moving, a voice said beside her without a hint of irony.

It took a few seconds for Erica to realise that the voice belonged to her girlfriend.

8

2019 / LONDON

They had been blessed by the gods of the M6, and made it to Liverpool by eleven a.m. sharp. It could have been sooner, but Joy insisted they stop to let Bernie stretch his legs halfway through the journey. He hadn't moved an inch since promptly falling asleep when they set off from London, but Joy spotted a sign for a McDonalds at a service station and couldn't resist the siren song of hash browns.

The traffic in Liverpool grinds them to a halt in the city centre, a few minutes out from the hospital. Seb taps the steering wheel impatiently. Joy has no more conversation left to make. She slurps the dregs of her Fanta through the paper straw, now a soggy mess. She doesn't let her teeth touch it, can't stand the feeling. Seb shoots a look sideways at her. She stops slurping. The cars ahead of them edge slowly forward.

Must be some roadworks or something, Joy ventures.

Mm.

We're not far off now, anyway.

Mmhm.

She doesn't bother trying again. Eventually the traffic gives way and they make it to the multi-story car park of the Royal Hospital.

Right, Seb says, let's go find her.

I – Joy starts, *we* can't leave the dog in the car by himself.

Seb grips a handful of his hair in his hand and exhales hard.

Fine. *I'll* go. You stay here, do whatever you want.

Don't be like that, you know we can't leave him in here. I'll go for a little walk with him, just call me when you find her room and let me know what's going on.

Seb nods wordlessly and exits the car, throws the keys into her lap. Joy sits for a few minutes in silence before gathering herself. Liverpool. Back in Liverpool. Somewhere outside of this car park, Erica is walking around living her life, unaware of Joy's presence in the city.

She looks out of the front window; all that surrounds her is cars and strip lights. The dreaded thought of spending an unknown number of days or weeks with her mother-in-law makes her shudder. She calls Bernie's name; his golden head pops up from behind the back seats. She softens immediately, can feel a small amount of anxiety leave her body. She releases him from the boot and clips his lead on, they head out of the car park and onto the street.

Before she has time to formulate a route in her head, an old man with a thick scouse accent stops her to ask the time and if he can fuss Bernie. He makes polite conversation about the weather as he scratches her dog's ears. His accent feels like a familiar pair of fluffy slippers. She resists the urge to tell him that she is from here, that she used to sound a little like him, that she knows she sounds like an outsider, but she isn't. She talks about the weather instead. He tips his cap as he says goodbye. Joy's spirits lift. She has forgotten how friendly people can be up north. If you tried to stop somebody in London for anything as trivial as petting a dog or asking for the time, you'd all but be hissed at.

She leads Bernie to a small patch of grass near to the car park and lets him sniff around. She inhales big gulps of northern air. Even with the fumes from the nearby main road, it smells fresher than London. They amble around for a while, unwinding from the long car journey, Bernie sniffing at every lamppost, occasionally looking up to check that his mother is still there. Joy's phone buzzes with a call in her back pocket, she lifts it to her ear.

Broken leg, Seb says, they're discharging her tomorrow, she's off her tits on pain meds but she's okay, we just missed visiting hours. We can go back to hers now and get some rest before we pick her up tomorrow, get some shopping in and all that.

Right, erm, should I get the car ready, then?

Well, I'm hardly going to get an Uber, am I?

She hates it when he is sarcastic. Decides not to mention it, he is under a lot of stress.

Just get the car started and bring it round to the front of the hospital, okay?

The line goes dead.

She calls Bernie away from a tree stump that he has his nose buried in and walks him briskly back to the car park.

She rushes back up to the floor they parked on. The floor she thought they parked on. Joy curses at herself for not taking note of it when they got out of the car. It's so cold out, she doesn't want to leave Seb waiting outside the hospital for ages. She roams the second floor packed full of cars searching for theirs, but with no luck. She climbs the stairs to the third floor. Bernie is oblivious to her rush as he tries to stop and sniff every corner of the staircase. She finally spots their Range Rover, does a weird jog towards it. By the time she has Bernie back in the boot and has seated herself behind the steering wheel, she is sweating. Her phone vibrates again, Seb calling, she is taking too long. She drops it down the side of the driver's seat, can't fish it out. Panic starts to flood her body. She closes her eyes and takes three deep breathes, tries to control it. Her grip on the steering wheel turns her knuckles three shades paler. Bernie barks from the boot as a passer-by knocks on the window. They are saying something, asking something. She lifts her head and realises how tragic the scene must look in the car park of a hospital. She stretches a manic smile onto her face and nods at the person. They look concerned, but walk away, reassured that she isn't having some sort of heart attack or emotional breakdown. She laughs at herself. She hasn't been here for more than twenty minutes and already she is exhausted. The panic starts to seep away. A rare miss of a full-blown attack.

In her calmer state, she reaches down the side of the seat and retrieves her phone, calls Seb back. Immediate answer, no greeting.

Where are you?

I'm coming now I just-

Hurry up, it's bloody freezing.

I'm on my way.

Hurry up.

The line goes dead again. She takes a deep breath and reverses out of the space, follows the arrows out and creeps into the traffic leading to the entrance of the hospital. She wants nothing more than a cigarette and a giant wine, but neither of those things are available to her right now. She thinks about the emergency pack of Marlboro's she has in her bag, but there's no chance that Seb's bloodhound nose would miss the smell of it in the car. Not worth the hassle.

The car slowly makes its way towards the hospital entrance. Joy spots Seb standing with his phone in his hand, she checks hers, it's not her that he is texting. Phew. He spots her and walks towards the car, Joy hops out and gets in the passenger side, Seb always likes to be the driver. Bernie barks when he gets in.

Shut it, he shouts to the dog as he fishes for the seatbelt.

Joy shoves down the rage bubbling just under the surface. She knows that the dog can't understand what's being said to him, but that doesn't make it okay.

So, she says as they pull out of the hospital entrance, how was she?

Fine, they've got her on a lot of pain meds. Her friends have been in to drop magazines and some other stuff to keep her busy. One of them has taken her an iPad, as if Mum knows how to use a fucking iPad? She can barely use a microwave.

Joy laughs, relief washing over her as she glimpses a flash of her relaxed and funny husband. He's definitely still in there somewhere.

They spend the journey to Formby making a shopping list and planning the rest of the day. As they pull into the driveway of Margaret's house, Seb's phone pings from its place in the Sat Nav holder. Joy glances at the screen and see's Valencia's name.

Val?

Ah, he grabs the phone from the plastic holder, yeah, I text her earlier to let her know we're back.

Oh, Joy says, I was going to make it a surprise.

What, us being back to look after my Mum? Hardly a great surprise.

He taps away at the screen. Is he tilting it away from her? She is being paranoid, probably.

Shall we grab the stuff then?

Sure.

They exit the car and release Bernie from the boot. He immediately goes to investigate the front lawn and cocks his leg up a small cherub statue by the large front door. Margaret would go mental if she saw that happen. Joy likes to think that he does these things in solidarity with her.

Seb opens the front door with his spare key and they dump the bags in the hallway.

Joy looks at her phone, just gone midday. How is it not yet an acceptable drinking hour? A text pops up on the screen from Valencia.

You're back! When are we seeing each other?! I'll save you from the dreaded MIL.

Joy smiles at the screen, letting a wave of excitement wash over her at the thought of making plans in Liverpool with her old friends.

She's not being discharged til tomorrow, thankfully. When are you free? X

Seb pushes past her to the kitchen, opens the fridge.

There's sod all in here, he shouts to her in the hallway.

She knows that that is a thinly veiled request for her to go and do a shop. Her phone buzzes again.

Friday eve? Take you for a drink!

Perfect, see you then x

Joy pockets her phone, already feeling brighter about the trip. Seb walks back into the hallway and throws his hands in the air.

There's no bloody food in this house. How does she normally eat? Is it a meals on wheels situation, do you think?

Joy laughs at his joke but knows not to overstep. The hunger induced anger isn't a fun one to deal with.

I'll go to Tesco now, send me a list of what you want. Also, Val just text, I'm gonna get a drink with her on Friday, is that cool?

Seb shrugs and heads into the living room. Joy hears him turn on the TV, the unmistakeable sound of a football match filling the silence.

Get some beers too, he shouts from his new position on the sofa, feet on the coffee table.

Joy fishes Bernie's water bowl out of her bags and fills it up for him, he bounds inside the house and finds a spot to settle. She ruffles the fur around his ears before she leaves, attempting to take some of his lovely happy energy with her into the outside world.

It has been years since she has visited Liverpool, let alone driven around it. There is a supermarket five minutes from Margaret's house, but she drives to the multistorey car park of the Big Tesco's in L1, right on Hanover Street instead. The one-way systems of the city centre are a nightmare, but she braves them, needlessly, just to see what it all looks like now. Stepping onto the street, she remembers the energy of the city immediately.

A car is forced to halt in the road next to her, the obstacle of five colossal seagulls fighting over a half-eaten bag of chips in its way. The sound of the horn does nothing to deter them. Joy remembers how Erica used to liken her to a seagull, for both her tenacity when she wanted something, and the animalistic way in which she would eat chips. She rubs her thumb over the faded outline of the tattoo on her wrist as they take flight, dragging what is leftover of the bag with them, showering chips all over the pavement.

*

A group of students dressed to impress stroll past her, arms linked. It's the end of September, and although the sun is shining, it's absolutely Baltic. Yet they are walking to their boozy days out wearing nothing but short dresses and impossible heels. Joy remembers that sort of confidence, the total disregard for the weather forecast. She looks down at herself, the shape of her body unrecognisable under her big winter coat. Despite her relatively young age, she somehow feels ancient. Living a life beyond her years, slowly crawling closer to thirty and living like she is already retired.

She makes her way through the entrance to Tesco's and grabs a trolley. She has no idea what food Margaret likes, so she will just have to guess. Hearts of the innocent, perhaps? She throws some of Seb's favourites in there; sausages, bacon, a few different cheeses, some ready-made pizzas, tosses in some fruits for good measure. At least they'll look nice in the fridge as they inevitably rot away. She heads for the frozen vegetarian section, grabbing croissants and some jams on the way. She is planning dinner in her head when her trolley collides with another coming round the corner of the home baking aisle.

Shit, sorry, a voice says.

She would recognise that voice absolutely anywhere. Her heart leaps into her throat as Erica's bunched up bright orange hair comes into view; a huge pair of black rimmed glasses sitting on her freckled nose. It takes a moment for her to register that Joy is standing in front of her.

Fucking hell, she says, black painted lips in the shape of an O.

Nice to see you too, Joy laughs, instantly regretting leaving the house looking like something that asks you to solve a riddle as you try to cross a bridge.

The girls abandon their trolleys and embrace in the middle of the gluten free section. How bizarre that this is happening? How utterly strangely coincidental that they should run into each other here? She holds Erica by the shoulders and examines her face, as if to make sure that she isn't some sort of fabrication of her imagination.

Wow. You look different. She takes her in, still ginger, still wearing their old trademark black lipstick, a flannel shirt with the sleeves rolled up, way more tattoos than the last time Joy saw her.

Yeah, age and wine will do that to you, Erica laughs. And look at you, Mrs Married, Erica grabs Joy's left hand and examines her rings. Never thought I'd see the day.

Joy pulls her hand into the sleeve of her coat, can feel her cheeks turning red.

Me neither, she says quietly.

So, you're back then? Were you not going to tell me?!

No, of course I was. We literally got back like a few hours ago, Seb- my husband's mum has broken her leg. Gotta stay and make sure she doesn't break anything else.

Lucky you, that should be fun.

A wicked grin creeps onto Erica's face. Joy mock punches her arm and pulls a face.

It's so weird that you're here, like, in person, Erica says, shaking Joy's shoulder to see if she is real. Joy forces herself to ignore her stomach flipping.

Tell me about it, you just exist on my Instagram these days.

The pair laugh, their natural ease with each other returning fast.

And you're here shopping, obviously?

Yeah, I only live round the corner now. I'm actually here with-

Baaaaaabe, a high-pitched voice attached to a girl with long false eyelashes on rounds the corner holding a pack of lemons in her hand.

How many calories are in lemon water, do you think?

She looks up from her lemons and clocks Joy, recognition on her face.

Oh... Joy?

Yep, hi, Frankie. Nice to meet you in person. Joy does a weird little wave, which she regrets instantly, can feel her body temperature rising under the weight of her coat.

Yeah, super fun. She drops the lemons into their trolley and links a tanned arm through Erica's. What're you doing in Liverpool?

She sounds almost accusatory with her tone, as if Joy didn't grow up here.

I was just explaining to Erica, Joy says, my husbands' mum has broken a leg, we're back to take care of her for a while.

The plastic surgeon, right? She asks.

Yep, that's the one.

She nods in some sort of approval and heaves a big sigh, letting the awkward silence hang heavy.

I'll let you guys go, Joy says, but I am actually going out for drinks on Friday, if you wanna come? Both of you? Could be fun.

Erica goes to respond, but words leave Frankie's mouth before she can answer.

We're busy, I think.

Oh, no worries, it'll just be me and Val then.

Frankie double takes.

Val?

Yeah.

She thinks for a moment. Maybe we are free, I'll check. We'll let you know.

Frankie flips her blonde curls over her shoulder and directs Erica and their trolley away towards the fresh produce.

Erica looks back and rolls her eyes. Joy watches them walk away together; the conversation looks slightly heated. She knows that Frankie has a problem with her, doesn't like Erica talking to her via Facebook, let alone randomly in their local supermarket. They seem an oddly matched couple. Since Erica and Frankie got together, Joy has only been able to view their relationship through the rose-tinted glasses of social media posts. That, plus Val's scathing opinion on their pairing has led to mixed reviews of them as a couple. She hopes that Erica will come on Friday. Wonders if there is any way that could happen without Frankie and her passive aggression attached. Doubts it.

She whips out her phone to text Val.

Just bumped into Erica and Frankie. What are the chances?!

She shrugs it off and grabs some veggie burgers and sausages from the freezers in front of her, piles them into the trolley absentmindedly. For all the drama that could have been their reunion, a strained conversation in Big Tesco's did it.

A reply pings straight back, Val must be constantly glued to her phone.

That's so spooky! Was it awks?

Kind of, given that Frankie hates me lol. Nice to see Erica though. They might come on Friday, hope that's okay x

Any shopping list that she had memorised is gone. She looks at her trolley, it looks like what she used to buy at uni. Just a bunch of comfort food and some apples for show. She quickly traipses round the rest of the store throwing in actual things to cook with, along with a few bottles of wine and a crate of beers for Seb. She checks out using his debit card, can't remember the last time she had her own money.

As she piles the shopping into the car, her phone buzzes again. Quite a long response time for Val. She taps the screen, but instead of Val's name, she sees Erica's. She swallows hard and opens it.

Let me know where to be and when on Friday.
So glad you're back x

Joy stares at the message for a moment, just as the phone comes to life in her hand and she almost drops it.

Hello?

Where are you? The dog is whining.

Ah, he probably wants a walk. I've just finished shopping so won't be long.

Mmhm.

Seb hangs up the phone and she climbs into the car, rests her head against the steering wheel. Takes a deep breath, starts the engine. She needs to get back.

She drives away from the city and back towards her husband, the outline of her seagull tattoo staring up at her from the wheel.

*

The nap she took when she returned to the house has filled her with grogginess. She pours herself a large glass of wine to try to combat it, checks the map on Deliveroo again to see if their driver is any closer. They ordered the pizza at seven, almost an hour ago. She hasn't stopped thinking about it since. She pours a glass of red for Seb and takes it to him in the lounge. The last time they had takeaway food was so long ago that Joy struggles to recall it. Seb sighs beside her.

Where's this bloody pizza?

On the way, she says, looking at the map on her phone, the little animated car getting closer and closer to them.

We should have just cooked, he says.

The way he says 'we' gets under her skin. Aside from the odd bit of toast, he hasn't cooked for her since they were first going out. Even back then it was spag bol out of a jar, but she appreciated the effort still.

I'm just too tired to cook, sorry.

I know, that's why we've ordered pizza, no need to get mardy.

I'm not-

She is interrupted by the doorbell. Bernie gets to his feet and shouts at the front door. Joy tells him to sit, that there is no danger, thanks him for his concern. She can practically hear Seb roll his eyes, he's never understood why she talks to the dog like he's a person.

Joy retrieves their boxed dinner from the long-haired teenager at the door, politely ignoring the strong smell of weed emanating from him. He nods a hazy thank you as she closes the door behind her.

The smell of hot melted cheese makes her stomach growl. Pineapple pizza, her all-time favourite. She has been made fun of mercilessly for this, of course. The never-ending debate of pineapple on pizza a favourite topic of conversation amongst well-meaning friends.

She carries it back into the living room and opens the box up on the coffee table. She runs to the kitchen to pull some nachos out of the oven that she'd made earlier. Sprinkling grated cheese onto tortilla chips counts as cooking, kind of, right?

Seb dives into his half of the pizza, meat feast, his favourite. Sometimes, when she was hungover in uni, she used to make him hold a slice and let her sniff the pepperoni, like a junkie gone cold turkey. They pour themselves more wine. He hands her the remote and they happily munch away whilst watching an episode from season four of Sex and the City. Joy used to be obsessed with the show. Seb mocked her endlessly for it, but eventually got sucked into the storylines. He likes Miranda the most, although Joy maintains that Samantha should be everybody's favourite. He calls it his guilty pleasure, but she knows full well that if she were to mention that in front of his friends, he would deny all knowledge.

A few hours later and the pizza box lies empty in front of them. Bernie snores loudly from his chosen spot in the kitchen, and the TV is stuck on the irritating 'are you still there?' screen that Netflix throws at you when it deems you have watched an irresponsible amount of one show. Joy wakes abruptly from her booze induced sofa snooze to find herself tucked under an unconscious Seb's arm, his glass of red wine limp in his hand, its contents dribbling onto the sofa. She considers getting up, fishing out baking soda and whatever cleaning products might be in the kitchen to rescue the furniture, but doesn't. She settles back into her spot, muscle memory creating a kick of serotonin in her brain as her body remembers all the times she has lay in this position, on this part of her husband. She tries to recall the last time they lay like this. The last time they both had an evening free and wanted to spend it together. She can't think of it. This just isn't something they do anymore. Granted, he is unconscious and doesn't know it's happening, but she savours the moment anyway.

He stirs suddenly, swearing quietly as he notices the red wine bleeding from his glass, slowly staining the sofa.

Passed out with a red wine before eleven, wow, how old are we now? He laughs and rubs his tired eyes.

We? Don't lump me in with you, mister. I'm still in my twenties, you're the ancient one. She pokes his ribs.

He lightly pushes her arm and sets his glass on the coffee table, leaning over her to do so. She breathes him in.

Mum will go mad when she sees this, he says as he pokes the red wine spill. Better try and get rid of it. He goes to get up, but Joy holds onto his hand, this sudden rare wave of affection for him surging through her.

Leave it, I'll do it tomorrow, let's just go to bed.

Bed? He looks at her, questioningly, recognising her tone.

Bed, she says, not breaking eye contact.

The stain lies abandoned, the wine left to soak further into the fibres of Margaret's beige sofa, as they chase each other up the stairs in a haze and slam the bedroom door behind them. In a half drunken frenzy, they tear clothes from each other, becoming a mess of tangled limbs, bitten lips and breathy laughter. Joy had almost forgotten what her husband felt like, the weight of him on top of her, the sensation of having him inside of her so familiar, yet alien after so long. She lets him bend her into positions that they haven't attempted in years, makes the right noises when he pulls her hair and demands she say his name.

Afterwards, he holds her close to him. They fall asleep wrapped up in each other sweating and satisfied, like the young lovers that they once were.

*

Joy wakes the next morning with a foggy head and dry mouth. She peels her eyes open, her eyeballs immediately assaulted by the morning sun coming through the blinds. She rolls over, Seb is still out cold next to her. Her phone display tells her it is half seven, Bernie will be dying to go for a wee. She carefully creeps out of bed and pulls her dressing gown out of one of the suitcases that are in disarray on the floor. Wraps it around herself, takes a moment to survey her sleeping husband before she leaves the room. They haven't had a night like that in a long time, perhaps things are changing between them, she thinks.

She decides she will prepare them a big breakfast. They can enjoy it together before he has to go and pick up his Mum and the strange new bliss is ruined. Joy opens the bedroom door as quietly as she can as not to wake him and is greeted by Bernie's golden face. He must have been there all night, so used to sleeping in the bedroom with her.

Sorry, baby, she says to him.

He tilts his head in response.

You want some breakfast? And a wee-wee?

He licks her hand, she kisses his furry forehead, directs him to the stairs.

They plod into the open plan kitchen together and she releases him out of the back door, he immediately relieves himself up against one of Margaret's treasured garden ornaments.

Good boy, she says under her breath as she attempts to understand the coffee machine that rests on the kitchen island. She feels a particular type of satisfaction as she grabs milk out of the fridge, almond and regular. Stares ahead dreamily as she stirs everything together and slides fresh bread into the weird see-through toaster. It doesn't have a dial or push down buttons, but a screen. Where did Margaret get this? No wonder the woman never cooks, her appliances aren't boomer-generation-friendly. She prods at the screen and sets something called 'degree of toastiness' to a golden-brown colour, it pulls the bread in by itself. Magic. Joy wants one immediately. Looks it up on her phone. Amazon, £215. Fuck off.

She sips at her coffee and pulls bacon and a vegetarian alternative from the fridge, heats up pans to fry them till crispy. Heats up beans, adds butter and herbs, a trick she learned in Uni to make them extra tasty. Scrambles some eggs, extra for Bernie. Just before everything is ready to be plated up, she shouts for Seb to come downstairs.

The steaming plates of breakfast food sit next to each other on the island, his coffee waiting for him at a drinkable temperature. Joy fills Bernie's bowl with his regular biscuits and the extra scrambled egg, he eats with pure happiness and promptly falls asleep. She hears Seb's footsteps.

Do we have any painkillers? He opens a cupboard and rummages through it.

I have some in my bag I think, hang on. She skips out of the kitchen and rummages through her handbag in the living room, smiles at the state of how they left it. A reminder of their rare spontaneity. She locates a pack of paracetamol, hands them to him as she enters the kitchen again.

Here, get them down you. I made us a fry up, thought it might be nice to eat together.

She smiles at him, waiting for recognition that he is feeling the same as she.

Hmm? Oh, thanks. I'll have to be quick though, got some bits to do before I go get Mum.

Oh, she says, taken aback, bits?

Just some stuff for work, the Rodney Street office need an extra pair of hands while I'm here, not like I can say no since they've just let me take some leave from London.

But if you've taken leave, shouldn't you like… be on leave?

Christ, Joy, I'm up here and they need some help, so I said I would do it. Problem?

No, no. I got your favourite bacon yesterday, she gestures to the plate.

Yeah, thanks, he says whilst typing into his phone.

She swallows hard.

Last night was really fun, she ventures.

Mmhm, he sips the coffee and winces. This is yours, he says, and hands the mug to her.

Sorry.

She sits at the island and dejectedly picks at her scrambled eggs. Any hopes she had of a romantic post-sex-bliss morning are slowly eking away.

He stands for a while longer tapping away at his phone.

Your food is getting cold, she says.

Huh? Oh, yeah. He picks up his fork and stabs a few pieces of bacon into his mouth, puts on his shoes and picks up a piece of toast to take with him.

Thanks, see you later.

When are you coming back? She immediately regrets the words, hates coming off as needy.

He turns to her and puts his phone away, but she can hear it vibrating in his pocket.

I'm picking Mum up at four, we'll be back just after that. Remember she doesn't like spicy food or anything that sounds Mexican, and make sure you get that stain off the sofa.

He says it with nothing in his eyes, as if that stain doesn't indicate the most romantic evening they have had in ages.

Sure, I'll do what I can. She starts to clear up the breakfast plates, scrapes his wasted food into the bin, stacks the plates into the dishwasher loudly.

And keep the dog off the furniture, he shouts, his voice muffled from the toast he has between his teeth. He briefly kisses her on the head before leaving the room.

He pulls his coat on and shouts goodbye from the front door, and just like that, he's gone.

She stands for a moment, staring at the spot he just left.

Her phone buzzes from the kitchen island. The screen announces that she has been put into a group chat.

DRINKS ON FRIDAY

She inspects the group participants. Hosted by Val and includes Joy and Erica. Her stomach does a strange little drop, she is immediately taken back to running into Erica at the shop yesterday. Her orange hair, her thick glasses, those freckles that were always so prominent after the summer months. Frankie's shitty attitude. She is grateful that Val didn't include Frankie in the group chat. Doesn't want to have to pretend to like her more than she needs to. A message pings through.

Val: Heya queens So, for Friday, I was thinking Chamber 36 for some Chinese food? Then maybe down the road to petit café for some fancy pants wine and jazz that we can pretend we're cool enough to like? xo

Joy can't help but smile at the screen, her mood immediately lifting.

Joy: Sounds amazing. Just let me know the time and I'll be there x

She makes a mental note to message Val separately and ask if Frankie is going to be joining them. Or would that be weird? Or obvious?

Val: Perf, let's say 7pm? I'll book it now. E, is Frankie coming? Xo

Joy can see that Erica is typing a response. The butterflies in her stomach respond to seeing her name with urgency.

Erica: She's got plans with that hoard of cackling twats that she hangs out with; said she'll meet us at some point.

Val: HA! Amazing, will be great to catch up all together anyway. See you then babes <3 xo

Joy laughs out loud into the silence of the kitchen at Erica's message. She has missed her dry sense of humour. Suddenly the day doesn't seem as shitty. Not long until she gets to hang out with the girls, feel like herself again. She plays Bauhaus through her phone speaker and tidies the rest of the kitchen up. Takes a bunch of cleaning supplies through to the living room and scrubs at the stain, tosses away the bottles and boxes, rearranges the many pointless sofa cushions. She heads out into the crisp air of the garden to throw a ball for Bernie. The whole day stretches in front of her. She pulls a cigarette out of her pocket and lights it. The battered neon smiley face painted onto it stares back at her, as it always has since she acquired it from Erica all those years ago.

9

2013 / BRIGHTON

Erica's stomach rumbled. She did her best not to snatch the hot paper bag full of deep-fried McDonalds goodness out of the servers' hand, it wasn't their fault that she was starving. She opened it and stuffed some fries into her mouth. The satisfaction was immediate, she slurped at a cold coke in between mouthfuls. She joined their group sitting on a table outside of the bar they had been in since the exhibit ended, laid out her food on a napkin and made her way through all of it. She knew without glancing upwards that Joy's new friends were looking at her in disgust. She didn't understand how they weren't ravenous. Joy sat beside her and stole a fry from her makeshift picnic blanket.

Want a bite of my cheeseburger, babe?

Oh, no thanks, I don't eat meat anymore, remember.

Erica nodded a little and finished the burger by herself, after extracting the pickles.

Joy had taken her aside when bitesize pieces of questionable looking fish were being circulated at the exhibition, told her that she doesn't eat meat anymore, and not to mention to her friends that she wasn't vegetarian before.

I can't believe how much people like that stuff, Pink Dreads Girl says from her seat opposite Erica, her pupils wide.

Same, said Blonde Girl, its poison, far better to stick to a plant based, organic diet.

The others nodded along.

Erica doesn't eat much meat, Joy said from beside her.

I do, actually. I know I need to cut down. But cheeseburgers are delicious, aren't they? She laughs, but none of them laugh with her.

Erica couldn't even muster up the energy necessary to care what they thought of her at that point. She had spent the day hungry, being dragged around various sticky pubs and that weird exhibition. Her bag still hadn't been deposited in Joy's halls; she hadn't spent more than two minutes alone with her. It's okay, she kept telling herself. Joy is just excited about her new friends. She thought that perhaps it would be much the same for her when she started here next year. Although hopefully with nicer people. They still had the whole weekend stretched out in front of them, and as soon as they got back to Joy's room, she knew it would be just like always.

She finished her McDonalds and tossed the packaging into a nearby bin.

Shall we get going soon, babe? Erica hoped the desperation in her voice wasn't too noticeable.

It's only nine thirty, Huge Glasses Guy said, rubbing at his nose.

Yeah, said Pink Dreads Girl, we have this cool like, underground place we like to go. We've got a bag for the occasion.

A bag? Erica asked, dumbly.

They cackled as a group, Joy looked torn as to who her loyalties should lie with. She chose to sip her drink instead of saying anything.

Cocaine, hun. Come on, Joy tried it last week and loooooved it.

Erica looked at Joy, she wouldn't meet her eyeline.

You did drugs?

Well, it was just a bit, for this rave thing we went to.

You didn't tell me?

Awh come on, Erica, it's not a big deal, said Blonde Girl.

Yeah, it's just a bit of fun, chill out, jeeeeez, Pink Dreads Girl said, pulling a key out of her pocket and dipping the tip of it into a small bag of white powder and lifting it to her nose. Erica watched it disappear with a sharp sniff.

Joy stood up and led Erica away from the group, trying to hold her hand, which she batted away.

What's going on with you? Erica said.

What? Sorry I didn't tell you; I just knew you wouldn't be into it.

Not just that, Joy, you're like a totally different person.

Don't be so dramatic, babe.

I don't think I'm being dramatic; I think you're being weird. You're acting like some total posh asshole, like them. Erica pointed her thumb behind her in the direction of the table.

I'm just making friends, please don't be jealous.

Jealous?! I'm not jealous, babe. They're awful, they've been really condescending to me all day and you don't seem to care. Since when do you do drugs? And also, what's happened to your accent? You sound really odd.

Joy pulled a cigarette out of her pocket and lit it, aware that her friends were staring at them both from the table, waiting for a scene to happen.

It's just easier than dealing with all the 'thieving scouser' jokes. She looked at her feet.

People have said that? Erica asked, a protective hand on Joy's arm.

Joy nodded.

Oh, my love, I'm sorry. It's just not the weekend I thought we'd be having. I missed you so much, I just wanted it to be us.

I know, Joy says, stubbing her half-smoked cigarette out on the sole of her shoe.

Erica took her hands.

Look, let's just get some drinks from the shop, head back to yours, watch some films, and then tomorrow you can show me the beach, yeah? Start fresh?

Joy looked at her, face softened, her brown eyes glistening with the threat of tears.

JOY?! One of the pack shouted from behind them.

Jooooooyyyyy?! Come on, we're going to The Arch, get your ass into gear. They cackled as they necked the last of their drinks and started to walk towards the club.

Joy looked torn; Erica could feel the grip on her hands pulling away.

No, babe, come on. Leave them, just be with me.

Erica pleaded with her eyes, but to no avail.

We're coming! She shouted.

She broke free from Erica's hands and pushed her hair back.

Come on, it'll be fun.

Joy bounced off towards her friends. She looked back, gesturing for her to hurry up. Erica motioned that she needed to grab her bag, that she would catch up.

She watched them throw their arms around each other, watched Pink Dreads Girl dig the small baggy back out of her pocket and pass it to Joy. She couldn't do it. What was the point of her being here? She had travelled the length of the country to see her girlfriend, and still didn't feel like she'd gotten to her. This person she'd spent the day with wasn't the one she knew, the one she loved. She couldn't face the idea of spending the rest of the weekend getting her heart broken minute after minute as she watched the woman she loved morph into an entirely new person. Joy looked back again; Erica gestured that she would be one minute. She went back to her friends as they made their way to the entrance of the club.

Erica turned the other way and walked towards the train station. Didn't look back. Got her phone out to text her.

Mum called, emergency, see you next time. X

She knew it was dramatic, but she wanted it to be. Joy could see the text and show up at the station to get her, a grand gesture of love reminiscent of romantic comedies.

As she sat in a seat on the 22:43pm train to London, she knew it wasn't going to happen. Tears came, and she let them. As the train pulled out of the station, a text came through from Joy.

What??? Where are you? Just come to the bar, you're being ridiculous.

Erica stared at the message. She couldn't bring herself to reply. Just switched her phone to silent and stared out of the window, watched the lights of Brighton become the lights of London, and longed for home.

10

2019 / LIVERPOOL

Joy sits back in the garden chair and cradles her glass of wine. Bernie brings the stuffed elephant back to her and drops it in her lap, she throws it for him again.

Good boy, she says, eternally grateful that this thing she loves the most doesn't judge her for day drinking.

She drains her glass and gets up, goes to the kitchen to check on dinner, shedding her jacket and blanket as she enters the centrally heated room. September has turned into October, and the chill up here is far worse than she remembers it ever being. The pot of slow cooked vegetable casserole simmering away on the stove emanates smells that remind her of home. Not hers, of course, but what she imagines home should have smelt like. Home cooked food, rather than stale smoke. She thinks of her dad as she stirs. Hasn't seen him in so long, perhaps she should drop in while they are here. Wonders if he even remembers that he has a daughter, let alone one that lives in London now.

She shakes it off, can't think of that right now. Must focus on dinner, on the imminent arrival of Margaret and her broken leg, on not letting on to Seb how many wines she's consumed. Lucky for her, she has always had her father's tolerance for alcohol. She pours herself a water and necks it, pops a polo in her mouth to mask the cigarette smell. Not that Seb doesn't know she smokes, he does, but he gives her a lecture every time he sees her with one. Also, she isn't sure she can withstand another talking-to from

Margaret about how smoke will harm her womb, thus possibly harming her chance of grandchildren. Despite always making her views clear on not wanting children, her mother-in-law has managed to ignore them completely.

Bernie bounds in through the gap in the bi-folding doors as noises from the hallway indicate that the front door is being opened.

No jumping, buddy, she says to him in a stern voice.

He stares back at her.

I mean it, she says, I know he's your dad, but he thinks you're a right dickhead.

She ruffles the fur on his head and takes a deep breath. The end of a foot appears in the doorway, wrapped in white cast and extended from a wheelchair.

For heaven's *sake*, Sebastian, watch my foot on the doorway.

Her accent still sounds like a person from the South attempting a scouse accent, or perhaps the other way around. Joy has never figured out which way she was trying to go with it.

Seb pushes her wheelchair into the hallway, looking exhausted behind her. Margaret's eyes flick up and down Joy immediately, no doubt doing mental aerobics to put together a rough figure of how much her outfit cost.

Darling, she says with a warm voice and cold face.

Hello, Margaret, how're you feeling? Joy leans down to kiss her on the cheek, the overwhelming and unmistakeable sickly scent of Mugler's 'Angel' dripping from her powdered pores.

Well, she gestures to the wheelchair, how do you think?

Joy laughs politely, unsure as to whether that was a joke, or an indication of how stupid she thinks Joy is. Best not to find out.

Bernie trots up to her, sniffs the wheels on her chair, then her jewellery laden hand.

Eurgh! She recoils her hand quickly, Bernie backs away.

That thing almost *bit* me, darling, bit me.

Mum, he didn't, he's nice, just annoying.

Joy grinds her teeth. Loops her fingers through Bernie's

collar and guides him back into the garden.

Sorry buddy, she says into his big brown eyes, don't listen to them.

She blows him a kiss and shuts the door behind her, plans on joining him as soon as is possible.

Hospital was a nightmare, Seb says as she re-enters the hallway. They took ages to discharge her.

You were the one that was late, darling, Margaret says, surveying the nails on her right hand, the location of the vicious dog attack.

You were late? She asks.

Seb ignores the question, pushes his mother into the living room. Joy notices him flick his head quickly in the direction of the sofa, checking to see if the stain is gone, no doubt.

What's for dinner? She asks in an authoritative monotone.

Joy has been cooking I think, Mum. Don't worry, I reminded her of all the stuff you don't like, spicy food and all that.

Yes, I've made us a vegetable casserole. It'll be really good for you, lots of veg and it's been simmering in red wine stock for hours, I made some bread too.

Joy feels proud of herself as she says the words. Never would she have thought when she lived in Brighton and ate nothing but microwaved crap and takeout that she would be capable of cooking much of anything, let alone her own bread.

Hmm, Margaret responds.

Joy shoots a warning glance at Seb, tries to make it known that she will not spend this entire trip being disrespected. He looks helplessly back at her.

I'm getting a drink, Joy says, anybody want one?

She walks back to the kitchen with the air of a stroppy teenager, but doesn't give a shit. They have been in the same room for precisely three minutes and already she wants to tear her hair out. She opens the fridge and pours herself a large white wine, takes a big sip, tries to calm down. Checks on Bernie, who is happily chewing on a stick in the garden.

Her phone buzzes in her pocket, bringing her back into the room.

Erica: Anybody know how to get fake tan out of literally every single pillowcase ever? Because, as you may have guessed, there is fake tan on every single one of my pillowcases EVER.

Joy laughs at the screen, unable to fully understand how Erica is in a relationship with somebody so opposite to herself. Never thought she'd see her with a girl who actively uses fake tan. They had always been quite proud pale goths.

Val: Tried throwing out the girlfriend? Lol xo

Erica: Wow, uncalled for haha.

Val: U know I'm kidding. Love that little oompa Loompa. xo

Erica: As if yours is natural, V!

Val: Girl, mines from St Tropez the place, not the bottle. xo

Erica: Hahahah, you absolute bitch.

Joy watches their back and forth on the group chat as though she is watching two strangers have a conversation. She knew that they reconnected when Val moved back to Liverpool, that they've been friends since, but it hadn't occurred to her that they might be this close. A strange type of envy flows through her.

Joy sends a laughing face emoji, doesn't have anything else to contribute. If she slates Frankie, it will come off as bitter.

Val: How's the dreaded MIL, Joy? xo

Joy: She just got here, nightmare already, considering poisoning the dinner.

Erica: Noooo, then you'd have to leave again, you're far too pretty to survive prison.

Butterflies, predictably. Does that mean that Erica wants her here? Or simply that she doesn't want her to go to away for murder?

Joy: Don't worry, wouldn't do anything to jeopardise our night out haha. Can't wait.

Val: Good luck, babes. Xo

Erica starts typing then stops. Annoying. Joy watches the little bar at the top to see whether she starts again, but her name doesn't reappear. She tries to ignore the thrum of disappointment inside of her.

So, Seb says as he enters the kitchen, what've you been up to today?

Oh, not much. Cleaned up, removed the stain, walked the dog, started cooking, bla bla bla.

Yeah? Is that your first drink, then?

He nods to the glass in her hand.

Why? Does it matter if it's not?

He pulls a beer from the fridge and sniffs at the pot bubbling on the stove.

Just don't want you turning into your dad, that's all. Leave that, he gestures to the food, Mum wants to play cards.

She stares at his back as he leaves the room again, mouth slightly agape. Did he really just say that? Why did she just let him say that? She looks at the drink in her hand, sets it down by the sink. Not worth the hassle. Her phone buzzes again, the group chat, Erica?

Val: I can't Friday, told you, I'm going out xo

Clearly meant for a different recipient.

Erica: Oooooh, who's Val arranging a date with?!

The message shows as deleted almost instantly; she doesn't respond. Always so private about her love life, Joy feels a swell of affection for her. Hopes she has found somebody who makes her happy, finally.

11

2014 / BRIGHTON

The night out had been Val's idea. Announcing to the living room of their tiny flat that she was sick of sitting around watching Christmas themed rom-coms and eating takeaway food, she had insisted to Joy and their flatmate Megan that it was time for some festive fun.

I'm sick of you moping, she had said to Joy. Val had practically dragged the pair up from the comfort of their sofa blanket pile, shedding Ferrero Rocher wrappers as they went, and shoved them in the direction of their bedrooms to get ready.

Val was clad in a tight red sequined dress, a well-tanned Christmas bauble with long, chocolate coloured hair. Megan, who they had met during their first ever summer break from uni at their favourite local pub, pulled on jeans and a garish Christmas jumper, complete with sticky-out Rudolph nose.

You reckon you're gonna get laid in that, babes?

It's not what you wear, it's how you wear it, she said, as she slipped on a huge pair of glittery heels and threw her hair up into one of those effortless buns.

Val had tried to talk Joy out of her Doc Martens, but had failed.

These are my fancy ones, she had said.

Four hours later and they were well and truly pissed. Joy and Val happily dragged on cigarettes, their faces inches from each other as they huddled under a limp umbrella, laughing hysterically at something that probably wasn't that funny.

Can you believe this will be our second Christmas here? Mental, Val said.

I know. Things are so different, it's crazy.

Val knew what she was referencing, but didn't bring it to the surface, didn't want to spend another evening listening to Joy rehash the story of lost love and abandonment. It had been over a year since Erica had spoken to Joy. Val had tried so many times over the past year to fix her up with others. Get her mind off it.

Megan had been picked off two hours ago by a guy she fancied from her course. She took him back to the flat. Despite the awful jumper, it looked like she was the only one who was going to get any that night. Fucking finally, she had said to the girls, I thought he'd never take the hint.

Be safe, Joy had shouted above the thump of the music.

Megan had winked back, happily swaying to the beat as she made her way back over to the beige looking guy that they would inevitably have to listen to her shagging all night.

Joy and Val had continued the night by themselves, as they so often did, in a haze of shots and cigarette smoke. Some old hippies had offered them bumps of coke in the toilets, which they graciously accepted. This only fuelled the chatter emanating from their mouths, elevated the intensity of everything that they said to each other.

I need to quit smoking, Val said as she fished around in her soggy bag for another cigarette. Got a lighter?

Joy pulled her trusty neon smiley face out of her pocket, made sure she got it back.

Seriously, she said as she exhaled smoke, it won't look good on my socials, I'm starting to get serious followers, and smoking totally isn't cool anymore.

Joy looked at her in amusement, this statuesque goddess of a woman who consistently fretted over what strangers might think of her, when she was consistently the most beautiful human in any room that she entered. Madness, in Joy's eyes.

We can hit the gay bars if you like, Val suggested. About time you got back on the horse… or the… what's the lady equivalent of horse?

Joy smiled, it was nice of her to offer, but the thought of being with a woman who wasn't Erica made her stomach turn. Thanked the overlords of identity for blessing her with bisexuality, so that she may not be alone forever should she swear off of Erica-less women.

Don't worry, I'm just fine being the single-lady-horse that I currently am.

Val smiled and hugged joy with one damp arm.

Come on babes, let's get a sambuca.

As they turned to the entrance, Joy wrestled with the umbrella to get it down, swiftly hitting a stranger in the face with the sodden end of it.

Shit! I'm so sorry! Fucking thing, sorry… are you okay? Oh God, did I poke your eye out?

The eyes that met Joy's were a deep brown, and belonged to a movie-handsome face.

Movie-man smiled.

Don't worry, no eyes gauged out here.

Joy breathed a sigh of relief, unsure that she'd be able to handle the stress of a lawsuit in her second year of uni. She immediately clocked his accent, a hint of scouse, just like her. She had been working on losing her accent since she got to Brighton, but no chance hiding it after a couple of drinks.

I do demand compensation for my injured face though, he said, buy me a drink and tell me your name.

Val nudged Joy with her elbow and gave her a wink. She swayed past them and headed back to the bar. The look on her face said 'I'll leave you to it'.

Umm, okay, Joy did the nervous laugh that men always mistake as girlish laughter, but she is sure that most of the women that do it are just wondering how many ways this man could kill her if he so wished. And whether it is worth the gamble of a mediocre lay.

He didn't look like a murderer though, which was always a plus. He said his name was Sebastian, what a small world, he remarked when he noticed her accent. Sebastian is a posh boys name, Joy thought. They walked into the bar, his hand on her lower back. Intentions set. This would usually make her skin crawl, but not tonight. Electricity shot through her like it hadn't for a long time. She realised she had missed this flirty preamble. What had she been denying herself intimacy for all this time, anyway? Erica had clearly moved on, wasn't coming back, abandoned her for no good reason.

She ordered them two overpriced cocktails and they found an empty table in the corner. He looked at her intently as she spoke about herself, all but shouting in order to make her voice heard over the music. He was a few years older than her, a plus. She gazed around at the girls her own age being gyrated on by the guys in their same year at uni, barely able to handle their beer, clearly eyeing up the other girls as they attempted to get off with another. But not Sebastian. His attention was focused, he was only interested in her. Joy found herself reluctantly enjoying his gaze on her, not feeling overshadowed by Val's beauty for the first time in a long time.

Somebody was looking at just her.

12

2019 / LIVERPOOL

Valencia is woken by the sun beaming in through her satin curtains, illuminating the expanse of her bedroom. She wakes slowly, happily, stretches out her long limbs and flips her pillow over to the cool side. Enjoys the first few seconds of blurry consciousness before her list of things to do for the day seeps into her mind. It's Friday, finally. A wave of excited anticipation rolls through her body at the thought of having a night out. Lately, she has been staying in far more, tired of the stares when she visits popular places in town, the questions, the photo requests.

She opens her phone and sees a message from Seb. Doesn't open it. Seeing him a few days ago threw her off, an unexpected arrival back in her life. He and Joy have been at a safe distance down in London for a while now, and while she misses one of her best friends, she is glad of the distance. Joy would surely suspect things if they lived closer. She isn't stupid, would see it on their faces, or hers at least. Seb has always been good at hiding things. She tries to think of herself in a different light, but realises she has also kept the secret all these years, snuck around behind her back. She is no better.

Her excitement for the day is quickly replaced by shame, guilt. She squeezes her eyes shut and tries to push the hazy memories to the back of her mind. Focuses on her phone instead. Opens Instagram, checks her notifications. There are lots, as usual. Last night she had posted a selfie in her hello kitty pyjamas, toned stomach on show, blurred fairy lights in the background. Forty thousand likes so far. She looks at the comments, fatal mistake. Only ever does this when she wants to feel bad.

OMG your soooooo perf!!! <3 <3 <3

Girly where are those pj's from please

ugly fat fuckin BITCH

please drop us your skincare routine!

UR THE REESON I'M VEGAN!!!!!! <3

no WAY you look like that in person hahaha fake bitch

as if u thought this was a good pic, hahahah wow

Val clicks the button on the side of her phone and sends it to sleep. Doesn't need to see anymore. She gets out of bed and opens the door to her en-suite bathroom, turns on the shower, waits for it to get hot. She submerges herself in it, her long dark hair sticking to her back as the water makes its way down her small body. She sits on the floor of the shower. Cries hard, pulls at her hair. When she gets out, she wants to avoid the mirror, but can't bring herself to.

The plush towel around her is keeping her safe, safe from her reflection, safe from her own thoughts, safe from the hundreds of people who leave nasty comments about her body on every photograph that she posts. How disgusting they think it is. She drops the towel and surveys herself in the mirror. Grabs at her stomach, managing to clump together a miniscule chunk of something that isn't muscle or organs. She squeezes it until it is sore.

She runs her fingers over the scars at the tops of her thighs, some ancient, some fresh. She takes three deep breaths and puts on her dressing gown, storms to the kitchen. She gets out a block of cheese, soft white bread and three bags of crisps. She throws half a pack of bacon into a hot frying pan, eats a kit kat chunky while it cooks, she lets the hot fat spit at her hands. Doesn't flinch. She butters slices of bread, slaps the greasy bacon in-between them and retrieves a litre of full fat coke from the fridge, makes a coffee in her favourite mug, takes it all over to the sofa and puts on the TV.

Before she gets started, she moves the food out of the frame and snaps a picture of the mug, the morning sun flooding her apartment through the sash window behind it. Writes a caption.

Good Morning my lovely followers! I love starting my day with some meditation, reflection, and a GIANT coffee! How about you? <3 #CoffeeAddict #SelfCare #VeganLife

Stuffs her phone down the side of the sofa, doesn't want to look at it. She counts the calories as she eats and washes it down with as much coke as she can. It hurts more than water on the way back up, but she doesn't care. After everything she has done, she deserves this.

She deserves this.

13

2014 / BRIGHTON

So, you're not going home at all? Not even for Christmas Day?

Nah, what's the point? Joy swiped on eyeliner as she replied to Val, large black flicks that had been her staple since her teenage years.

Why not?

Joy met Val's eyes in the mirror.

It was a misery visiting over summer, can't imagine it'll be much better at Christmas. Dad will spend the whole time leathered, hot boxing the living room with his junkie girlfriend, I'll be confined to the local pub. Really don't want to risk running into you-know-who.

Mm, the name of whom we shall not speak. The one that quite literally got away.

Joy gave her a look.

Sorry, babes. You know you're welcome at mine though, yeah? My mum makes the best dinner, although Formby can be a bit of a Tory nightmare. But it's super pretty at Christmas, you wouldn't even have to tell your dad that you're back in town. You know there's that party that Seb and his family will be at too, it could be fun?

Thanks, but really, I'm okay here. Meg's mum is taking me in for the day. You looking forward to going home? Seeing the family?

Kind of, Val shrugged as she pulled hair out of an old hairbrush. There are so many stuffy parties that we have to go to at the neighbours' houses. I have to make conversation with men called things like Alan about their gravel companies and watch their miserable wives try and muster up smiles.

Oh, the troubles of the wealthy. Joy fell back onto the carpet dramatically, hand to forehead.

Sod off, Val said. Your new fella is one of us, you'll be at those parties with him before you know it. Trophy wife.

Trophy wife? Joy laughed. Have you seen me? The most expensive thing in my wardrobe is a Pixies shirt from the eighties. I'm no trophy.

Don't be soft, Val said. He's clearly smitten. Hence the disgustingly pricey restaurant he's taking you to tonight. Man doesn't skimp out on a third date, does he? You might actually have to throw him a shag after this one, babes.

Joy threw a makeup brush in Val's direction, sprinkling pale dust over the carpet. She didn't worry, they had given up on getting the security deposit back after the infamous 'does spaghetti stick to the walls' incident a few months ago.

I'm just saying, better to know if he's any good in bed before you carry on.

Sod off. Go find me something to wear, I hardly think they'll let me through the door in my usual attire of Sad Teenage Chic.

Val bowed, yes m'lady, and stalked off to her bedroom to fish out the agreed upon black dress that Joy was borrowing for the evening.

Joy took a breath. Her third date. Her third date with a man. She hadn't dated a guy since her early teenage years. Enjoying being around Seb so much hadn't been expected, her attraction to him had blindsided her. The first person she had been interested in since Erica left.

Val re-entered the room holding up two dresses in front of her. The cute black one they had agreed upon, and a pink sparkly number with a plunging neckline.

Hmm, how will I decide? Joy scratched her chin.

Thought I'd try, at least, Val said as she handed over the black one.

Shoes?

Oh yeah, Louboutin's okay for you?

If that means 'not too high' in English, then yes.

Val rolled her eyes and left to dig out a pair of heels under the six-inch mark. Joy slipped the dress over her head and surveyed herself, a different person, grown up. She wasn't sure that she liked it. But she knew Seb would.

Woooooow, you look so hot in that! Val said from the doorway. He's gonna go mental for you.

Joy shuffled a little, pulled the dress further down her thighs.

I dunno… it feels a bit more like you, than like me?

That's because it's my dress, babes. Trust me, you look incredible.

Val stood next to her in the mirror and draped a tanned arm around her. Joy's eyes flicked down to Val's thighs, exposed in her pyjama shorts.

You're doing okay?

Always, babes.

If you want to talk, we can–

Take that look off your face and stop worrying about me, the second you see him you'll be grand. The restaurant is meant to be amazing, you love food, focus on that.

I do love food.

Exactly, you'll be fine. Let's go and have a wine before he picks you up, calm you down a bit.

Joy relented, knew that asking too many questions just closed Val up. She had noticed it more since they had moved into the flat together, the way that she counted the calories of every piece of food she put into her mouth, the fresh cuts, the quick bathroom visits after dinner. Didn't know how to help her, or if she even wanted help.

The girls stood in their shoebox kitchen sipping cold glasses of corner shop wine. Their glasses didn't match, not much in their kitchen did. They had cobbled together cupboards full of plates, cups, mugs, pots and pans from different charity shops when they moved in, saving their money for the food and booze.

They heard their front door slam as Megan entered and joined them in the kitchen, her hair in disarray, wearing the same clothes she left in two nights ago.

Fucking hell, you scrub up alright, ay? She nudged Joy's arm and pulled a loose cigarette out of her pocket. Who's got a light for me?

Joy instinctively reached for hers in her jacket pocket and handed it over.

Christ, how do you still have this? Megan held the lighter in her hand, the neon smiley face staring up at her. Megan went to pocket it, but Joy grabbed it back out of her hand.

Some of us are responsible, said Val, poking her manicured finger into Megan's ribs.

Pfft, says Miss throw-up-all-your-food over here?

Megan, Joy warned, don't be a bitch.

Sorry, sorry. Megan dragged on her cigarette, blowing smoke into space between them.

So, where've you been? Joy asked Meg, keen to change the conversation.

Ah, just that guy from my course with the hair, you know? The one that I think looks like Thor? But like, a budget version?

Mm, the girls mumbled in unison.

We went on a night out then I just ended up staying at his for a few days. I figured it was time to get gone, there's only so long you can get out of one pair of pants and I didn't want him thinking it's going anywhere since we're shagging around the festive period.

Wow, Joy laughed.

Such a thoughtful person, Val said.

Piss off, both of you, least I'm getting laid. She drained a glass of wine in two gulps and stubbed out her cigarette into their ceramic frog ashtray.

So, Chinese food tonight? She asked Val, I need noodles and a Kate Hudson marathon.

Val nodded, pouring them more wine.

Sorry I can't join, Joy said, Seb should be here any minute to get me.

Where's he taking you?

Somewhere called Sixty-Four Degrees, Joy said with a shrug.

Fucking hell, Meg spat out a little wine.

What?!

He's a student, right?

Well, yeah, but he's like, a grown up already. Not undergrad, and I think his family have money.

Wow, well that place is crazy fancy, expensive too. Hold onto this one, jeez.

I don't really need a guy with lots of money.

Don't be ridiculous, that's what we all need, Meg said. Unless you're lucky like this one over here, hot and loaded. She pointed a thumb at Val then grabbed her softly by the wrist.

Come on, Lenny, there's rom-coms to be watched and takeout to be ordered.

Joy watched Val's face recoil at the utterance of her most hated nickname, a cursed version of Valencia that only Megan took pleasure in using.

Oh, Meg shouted back from the living room, we're still on for Christmas Day, right? You're still coming with me? Mum's bought the nut roast.

Of course, Joy shouted back, tell her thank you.

Her phone buzzed on the table next to her, it must be him. She didn't want him coming up to the flat, with it's million dead plants and slight aroma of chips from the place downstairs, Megan no doubt interrogating him about the contents of his bank account.

She shouted goodbye to the girls, slightly envious of their familiar evening plans, slipped on Val's heels and left, taking each stair as carefully as possible. Really didn't want to break her neck before trying this fancy food.

The December chill hit her as soon as she opened the door to the street. Couples huddled together in big coats and groups of friends in party hats strode past her, all on their way to fun filled evenings, work parties, dinners, dates. Joy breathed in the crisp air and pulled her furry coat tightly around herself, let the festive vibes of her lit-up street fill her with hope for the evening. Some locals had taken the care of stringing fairy lights between the buildings, along with garish plastic light up Santa's and reindeers hung from lampposts. Her legs were already numb from the cold, the knee length dress giving her zero coverage. She jigged on the spot a little to warm herself up and searched the passing faces for Seb.

A car pulled up in front of the chip shop, black, shiny, not environmentally friendly. Her knowledge of cars was limited to the colour and how many wheels they had, but this one looked like it wasn't cheap. The backseat window rolled down, revealing Seb's face. His broad smile, sharp jawline, his cheek dimples, she felt warmer already. He got out and opened the door for her, she tottered over to the car as confidently as she could in the shoes and slid into the backseat.

He got in next to her on the other side, nodded to the driver wordlessly.

A driver? Seriously?

Not my usual, I promise, just for tonight so we can get merry.

And the car?

Mine. Well, Mum's, but mine.

Joy nodded, smiled, took a glass of something fizzy from him, clinked glasses. She thought that this must be the most movie like moment she had ever experienced. The drink was sweet, refreshing. He watched her as she sipped it, that same look in his eye that he had the first night they met.

At the restaurant, Seb told the driver that he would call when they were ready for him. Joy cringed a little, felt out of place, almost rude to this man who was being paid to do exactly what Seb was asking of him. She was painfully aware that any cab journey she'd ever splashed out on was paid for in coins, the vehicle always having a faint smell of wet dog inside.

She wondered if this was his usual tactic for dates, flash the cash, wowed them, impressed them all the way to bed.

He held out his arm for her, the doors of the restaurant were opened for them by a smartly dressed member of staff who took their coats as they entered. Seb gave his details, and they were escorted to a table in the corner. Cocktails appeared as if by magic, he had ordered them in advance. She was touched, but worried she would hate it, that she'd have to grimace her way through a bitter horrid drink.

Joy took the delicate glass in her hand, her black nail varnish chipped in places already, picking at her fingernails an anxious tick that she never quite grew out of, and sipped at the pink, glittering drink.

Cheers, he said, as he delicately clinked his glass to hers.

Raspberry, mint, a hint of lemon. This was no two-for-a-fiver cocktail from the sticky bars she frequented, this was how they were supposed to taste.

Seb excused himself to use the bathroom, tucked his chair neatly back under the table after he stood. Joy took her drink in her hand and sipped again, taking the opportunity to observe the other diners in the small dining room. An older couple just opposite them sat, unsmiling, as a waiter poured blood red wine into their glasses. He left their table, and they drank without a cheers, surveying their menus with disinterested faces. They must come to places like this often, Joy thought.

Next to them, a younger couple. They held hands across the table, giggling, they both poked with their free hands at what looked like herby lumps of slime.

Snails? The girl whispered conspiratorially. Why are we somewhere where there's snails?

The boy laughed with her as an older couple returned from the bar and joined them at the table. They unlinked their fingers and stopped giggling. Joy wondered which one of them the parents belonged to, was annoyed for them that their fun had to stop at their arrival.

Seb returned, his eyes seemingly full of relief that she hadn't done a runner while he was away from the table.

So, she ventured as he took his seat, you come here often?

Does that line ever work?

No, oh my god, she put her head in her hands. I didn't mean it like that, like, I meant, genuinely, do you–

Relax, he laughed, I know what you meant.

Joy felt her face flame, took a large gulp of her drink to cool herself down, tried to push down the swelling sense of anxious nausea in the pit of her stomach.

I've been here a few times with some friends from my PhD, the food is always impressive, and I like the staff.

Joy's eyes flicked over to the man who had let them in and taken their coats. She wondered how much he was paid for his position.

I've never been anywhere like this before, Joy admitted.

I thought as much.

Joy looked at him, didn't know whether to be offended or not.

Not like that, ah, I mean, because you're a student, you know? And–

It's okay, she said.

Christ, we're both off to great starts, ay?

She smiled; he wasn't wrong with his assumption. Whenever she and her friends went out for dinner, their most expensive venture was a pizza hut buffet, sometimes a Nando's if they were feeling extravagant.

We can't all be posh totty, Sebastian, she teased.

Okay, okay, he held his hands up in defeat. You're spot on. I guess I've just gotten used to going out with women a little more… like me.

Wow, so many compliments, she said as she fanned herself dramatically.

My foot is just getting further into my mouth, isn't it?

I'll have you know, sir, that I borrowed this dress from my fanciest mate, and I even wore shoes that don't look like they were pulled from the corpse of a man in combat.

I noticed, he said, eyes boring into hers. I like that you're different, I really like it, actually.

Oh, yeah? And what would your mother make of me, do you think? Your bit of rough? She kicked his leg gently under the table.

Oh, she'd love you, yeah. My dead posh Mum from Formby loves nothing more than twenty something goths who refuse to spend more than a fiver on a bottle of wine.

She tried to jab at him across the table, knocked over the salt shaker.

You can say it all you like, but you know that it all tastes the same, you posh wanker. She laughed as she spoke, a little too loudly. The parents of the teenagers on the table next to them looked over and glared disapprovingly. Seb held up a hand in apology, covering his mouth with the other to disguise his smile.

I can't believe you just said that in here, he chuckled.

Starting to see myself why I might be different to your regular standard of date.

I'm not complaining, he said.

They might, Joy whispered, pointing her fork at the table next to them.

At that, a waiter appeared holding plates in his hands.

Oh, we haven't ordered yet? Joy said.

It's a whole tasting menu thing, don't worry, you'll love it.

Joy eyed the dish being set down before her suspiciously. Shells full of white lumps, smaller black lumps on top of them.

Traditional oysters, the waiter explained, topped with algae pearls and a spoonful of beluga caviar. He nodded at them and disappeared.

Seb saw the panic on Joy's face.

Don't worry, you'll like it, I'm sure.

They look… slimy?

Don't focus on that, look, just like this.

He lifted a shell off his plate and tipped it towards his face, letting it pour into his mouth and swallowed it all at once.

Joy stared at the shells in front of her, gingerly picked one up. She smelled a waft of sharp salt and lemon as she lifted it to her face.

All in one, Seb said.

She nodded at him, took a breath, and tipped the contents of the shell into her mouth as he had. Like a tequila shot, she thought, just swallow it and move on.

The temperature of the oyster shocked her first, she hadn't expected it to be that cold, the surprise making it harder for her to let it slide down her throat. She choked it down, tasting fish, citrus, and something she couldn't quite put her finger on. She felt her eyes water slightly as it descended her throat, a shiver running down her spine at the effort of keeping it down.

So? He asked hopefully.

That was… erm, yeah, wow.

You hated it, he said, a statement rather than a question.

She took a large gulp from her water glass.

No, she said after swilling as much of the taste out of her mouth as she could.

No? So, you're gonna have the other?

The colour drained from her face as she peered down at the plate, one more of them staring back up at her.

I'm kidding, Seb said, give it here.

He took her plate from in front of her and transferred the contents of her shell into his, replaced the empty one back on her plate and set it back in front of her.

Thank you, she whispered.

He chuckled as he finished his and hers.

You'll like the next course, I promise.

Her stomach rumbled as she finished her cocktail, surprised at the arrival of an oyster and yearning for something substantial to eat.

The waiter cleared their plates away swiftly and replaced their cocktails with fresh ones, this time the colour of cloudy lemonade. She sipped at it, her mouth coming alive at the hit of lime and sugar.

I'm sorry, Seb said, honestly, I just thought this place would, like, impress you?

Don't say sorry, I'm so embarrassed, I've just never eaten those before.

I should have asked where you wanted to go, stupid of me, I just wanted to make a good impression.

It's our third date, you tit. You already made the good impression.

She gently touched his leg with hers under the table, his brow softened.

If you could eat anything in the world right now, what would it be?

Honestly?

Honestly.

A hot dog. Like one of those really tacky ones that you can smell from half a mile away down by the beach, you know? Man, they're so gross, but soooo good.

Never tried one.

Never?! You're missing out. You have to be careful not to eat them in the open though, obviously. Seagulls.

She said the last word matter of fact, as if it was common knowledge that you must fight street birds for your dinner. Maybe it was, Seb thought, marvelling at this beautiful confusion of a woman in front of him.

The waiter arrived at the table again, setting down square plates in front of them, a pile of ice supporting a hollowed-out apple. He lifted the lids at the same time as smoke arose from them, revealing a world of colours inside. Joy's stomach rumbled.

So here we have minced crayfish, blended with–

Seb stopped the waiter mid-sentence.

Actually, could we get the bill please?

The bill?

The bill.

But… there are still six courses to go, sir.

Yes, and I'll be paying for all of them, of course, but unfortunately an emergency has arisen at home that we must attend to. The children, you see, they've taken ill.

Oh, I see. Apologies, sir; of course, I'll get the bill for you.

The waiter hurried away behind the bar, poking frantically at the till screen.

The children? Joy asked, amused.

Seb winked, mischief in his eyes.

Finish that drink, gorgeous.

Joy's whole body flooded with relief at the realisation that she wouldn't have to eat anything else in this restaurant. She did as she was told and drained her glass, thankful that the drinks were delicious.

Seb pulled out his wallet, various cards peeking out from inside. He retrieved a matte black one and slipped it inside the card machine that the waiter presented.

Joy shuffled in her seat, wondering whether she should have offered to pay half, not that she could have.

With a flourish, the man from the door arrived at their table with their coats, helped them into them and hurried them to the door.

We hope to welcome you back soon, sir, madam.

Seb and Joy thanked him as they exited the restaurant, back onto the cold, bustling street outside.

Right, he turned to her. Where would one find this hotdog stand? I'll fight a thousand seagulls if I need to.

She put a hand on either side of his face, kissed him quick and hard.

This way, posh boy.

She grabbed his hand and pulled him down the winding road towards the beach front.

*

Good, right? Joy asked, picking a fried onion off of her lap and popping it back into her mouth.

Seb made muffled noises through the mouthful of the bite he had just taken.

I'll take that as a yes, Joy laughed.

They sat on a wall facing the sea, the bustle of bars and Christmas parties, huddled smokers and drunken sing songs happening behind them.

Seb swallowed the last bite of his hot dog, dabbed the mustard off of his chin with a thin paper serviette.

Fuck me, he said, that was good.

Joy nodded in agreement, keeping the last bite of hers safe in her napkin.

Man, I needed that, she said.

I'm sorry about tonight, Seb said, looking out to the water.

Despite having lived here for some years now whilst he studied for his PhD, he rarely came down to the beach, rarely enjoyed himself at all outside of his tight knit circle of friends.

Please, don't say sorry. If anything, I'm sorry I wasn't into that place. Maybe when I grow up a bit? She laughed.

Wow, way to make me feel old.

Ah, there's only like eight years between us. Would have been weird when I was fifteen, not so much now, she teased.

You don't need to be sorry about not liking it, I'm just glad you came out with me again.

Why wouldn't I have?

Just wondering when you're going to realise, you're far too cool for me, you know?

Shut up, she said, and placed her hand onto his.

They were silent for a moment then, both watching as the dark waves crashed onto the pebbles, slight glints of moonlight illuminating their movements.

You didn't finish your hot dog?

Oh, yeah, it's not for me. It's for them.

Joy nodded towards a pack of seagulls wandering the pebbled beach, huddled close together for warmth among the chill of the coastal breeze.

The trick, she said, is to throw it from far away enough so that you don't get shit on.

I'm learning so much tonight.

She pulled him up by his hand and unwrapped the greasy napkin, shredded the last of her hotdog into bits before taking them in her fist and launching them into the air towards the birds.

They swarmed immediately, squawking and hollering, pecking at the morsels that had wedged themselves between the rocks. More came to join at the sight of food, and soon they were watching the birds as they picked up the morsels, dropped some, flapped their wings in displays of dominance and superiority, some flying away with the pieces they had found.

He turned to her then, a hand on her cold, pink cheek, the other on the small of her waist. Wordlessly, he pulled her closer to him and kissed her, the noise of seagull calls drowning out everything else around them.

I like you, he whispered into the cold air between their lips when he pulled away.

I like you, too, she replied, as she pulled him in again, a feeling in her chest akin to that of the flapping of the birds' wings before them.

*

He had kissed her again at her front door, held her tightly as they said goodbye. He was going home to Formby for Christmas, but had promised New Year's plans with her. She had opened the door to the grotty stairs that led up to the flat and leant against it, a giddy feeling inside of her like she hadn't felt in a long time.

As the warmth of the flat spread to her, she kicked off the shoes that Val had lent her, only now realising how painful they had been all evening. She threw her coat onto the floor at the top of the stairs and opened the door to the living room quietly, not wanting to wake the girls if they had, by some miracle, gone to bed before midnight. She entered the room to the two of them lounged under one chunky weave blanket, surrounded by chocolate wrappers. On the coffee table lay half-finished boxes of Chinese food, and three empty bottles of wine lined up beside them. Another bottle was being passed between them, being used as an ashtray. How To Lose a Guy In Ten Days was at its midpoint on the TV.

Jooooooy, Meg said, arms outstretched to hug her, how was it?

Joy hugged her, avoiding getting burnt by the last of the cigarette between her fingers.

Amazing, actually.

The food was good? Val asked.

No, horrifying. Too fancy for me, we actually ended up eating hot dogs down by the beach.

Adorable.

No sexy sex time then? Meg asked.

Nope, not tonight.

Ooft, what a gentleman. Come on in here, she said as she lifted the blanket and gestured for Joy to get under it.

Just gonna get out of this dress, thanks for the lend, V.

No problem, babes, Val said hazily with wine drunk eyes, a relaxed smile stretched across her perfectly symmetrical face.

Joy quickly ran to her bedroom and changed into her pyjamas, rubbed at her face with a baby wipe and returned to the sofa, settled in-between them. Meg pulled some of the blanket onto her, handed her a half full bag of prawn crackers and a mug full of room temperature wine. Val leant her head on Joy's shoulder, drunkenly giggling at the film.

*

When Joy awoke the next morning, they were still in the same position on the sofa, the cold light of the December morning peeking through their flimsy curtains. She rubbed her eyes and checked her phone, a text from Seb lay there, received last night.

Thank you for a perfect evening, see you after xmas gorgeous x

She looked from the text to her sleeping friends either side of her, unsure, at that particular moment, how life could possibly get any better.

14

2019 / LIVERPOOL

Erica curses as she knocks her elbow with her knee, sending a smudge of black lipstick up towards her nose. This is the sort of minor inconvenience that could easily send her into a spiral of crying and breathily asking herself *what's the point?!* But no, no time for that this evening.

She carefully wipes the smear away with a makeup wipe, touches up the colour on her cupids bow. Smacks her lips together like she always saw her mother do growing up, doesn't really get why, but enjoys the sound it makes. She looks over from her spot on the floor in front of the full-length mirror to Frankie, who is sat doing her own face at her vanity desk.

You look cute, Franks.

Thanks. Frankie pats the rouge on her own lips with a dry tissue, achieving a look that she spent twenty solid minutes telling Erica that was *trending right now*.

What's your plan?

The usual, she swivels on her heart shaped seat to face Erica. The Florist for cocktails and a snack, then concert square for shots and dancing.

Frankie just described Erica's night out from hell. She smiles anyway.

Sounds great, honey.

Yeh. And you guys? You're going where?

Frankie tries to keep her voice casual, but Erica hears the

undertone. The subtle demand to know exactly where she will be drinking with her ex-girlfriend.

Chamber Thirty-Six for Chinese food I think, then over the road to the little French café for wines.

Eurgh, sounds like an old person's night out. Where's the dancing? Where's the *fun*?

I think that sounds fun. Erica looks down at her socks, pulls a thread out from one of them, snaps it off.

Frankie laces endless straps from her heels around her toned calves, stands up behind Erica to survey herself in the big mirror. She looks like a goddess. A tanned, blonde goddess. Erica looks at herself too, her orange hair pulled into a bun, the same eyeliner and lipstick combo she's worn since the age of eighteen. Next to Frankie, she feels alien, ancient.

Erica, babe?

Yeah?

Can you move? I can't see my shoes in the mirror.

Erica obliges and rolls to the side, watches her girlfriend snap multiple pictures of herself in slightly altered poses each time. Let's her eyes float around the bedroom. It doesn't look anything like it did before Frankie moved in. There are fluffy pillows everywhere, and somehow a crushed velvet armchair has snuck its way into the corner. Erica has to try not to recoil every time she feels it looking at her.

Wanna have a drink together before you head off? Erica asks. There's wine in the fridge.

Frankie is still engrossed in her phone.

Nah, better not babe, don't want to look bloated when I get there.

She leans down to where Erica is sitting on the floor and goes to kiss her cheek. Erica moves to aim for her lips, but Frankie pulls away.

Babe, you've got black lipstick on, don't *actually* kiss me.

Forgot, sorry.

Frankie air kisses her and tells her she looks pretty.

As Erica watches her girlfriend pick up a sparkly bag and wave her exit out of the bedroom, she realises how laughable their differences are. They could have a sitcom based on their lives. *The Princess and the Freak*. Something awful like that. She thinks back to when they first met. Frankie was beautiful and charming, cute and ditzy. Erica was drunk and lonely. Pathetic, but true.

She takes a deep breath and pulls herself off of the floor, heads to the kitchen for a drink before she leaves. The thought of eating makes her nauseous, too anxious to begin to even contemplate putting noodles into her mouth at the restaurant. She wonders if Joy is feeling the same. How many times, she thinks, has she played the scenario of them bumping into each other over and over in her head? For it to have just happened so out of the blue has taken her by surprise. Suddenly being able to see the dimples in her cheeks when she laughs, or the pristine haircut that hasn't changed since they met. Her stomach lurches. She gets herself a cider out of the fridge and cracks it open, takes three deep gulps.

At least Val will be there, she thinks. The buffer. Their unlikely friend in common. When Joy and Val left Brighton, Erica hadn't expected either of them to return, but Val did. They bumped into each other when Val came into her workplace for a second piercing in her ear, Erica recognised her straight away as the only one that was nice to her when she visited Brighton all those years ago. Also, from the many photos on Joy's social media of the two of them pissed up at Christmas markets, on the beach, at theme parks, always mid-laugh. They went for a drink after she got pierced and caught up. Val had become Instagram famous, an *influencer*, which was now her full-time job, a concept lost on Erica. She filled her in on what Joy had been up to the last two years, meeting Sebastian, moving to London with him, not starting a career, but becoming some sort of child free housewife.

Erica drains her cider and checks the clock, almost six, time to go. She pulls on her Harrington jacket and heads out into the October cold. Her apartment sits in the Baltic Triangle of Liverpool, an "up and coming area", meaning that one day very soon it will cost thousands to live here. For now, it's a collection of gin bars inside old warehouses with minimal lighting, and independent food places. She loves it here. A gang of lively students run past the entrance to her apartment building, whooping and shouting to each other that the next bar is two minutes away. She lights up a cigarette and walks into the night.

The restaurant is one that Erica is familiar with, a favourite of hers and Val's when they go out for food. The cocktails are delicious and the food tasty, the atmosphere moody. Erica stands outside of this familiar place now, frozen. She glances at the time on her phone, almost six thirty. She knows that Joy and Val will be inside already, both sticklers for being annoyingly early to everything. She pretends to be reading the menu by the door as a couple pass her to go inside, but makes the mistake of glancing inside after them. Val catches her eye at the bar, waves at her.

As she enters, Joy turns around in the barstool she is sitting on. Erica can feel her heartbeat in her throat. What deal, she wonders, was made and with which ancient deity, for Joy to still have this spell-like ability to enchant her without even speaking? She hasn't changed, not enough for Erica to notice, at least.

Val pulls Erica into a tight hug, a gesture that let's Erica know that Val and Joy have been here for at least one cocktail's worth of time.

Hey gorge, Val says, our table is ready, we were just waiting on you. I'll go and let the waitress know and nip to the loo. She saunters towards the bathrooms, leaving a trail of expensive perfume behind her.

Erica turns to Joy and smiles. She goes in for a hug, but Joy holds out a hand, jabbing Erica's stomach as she leans in.

Shit, sorry, Joy says, pulling her hand away and hugging her loosely.

Erica curses herself, of course she doesn't want to hug you, she thinks.

The waitress directs them to their table, a booth by the window, Val's favourite spot in the place.

So, how's babysitting?

Joy looks at Erica, confused.

I'm not sure what the term is for looking after one's crippled mother-in-law.

Joy snorts with laughter, emitting a singular pig noise before promptly covering her mouth with her hand.

I believe the term you're searching for is pain-in-the-ass sitting, Joy says when she stops giggling.

That bad, ay?

Not yet, but it'll grow old quite fast, I imagine.

How's Sebastian coping with it?

She sees Joy flinch at the name of her husband in Erica's mouth.

He's fine, seeing his old friends a lot while we're here. Luckily his family has got money, so we've paid one of those private care people to hang out with her some evenings, like tonight.

Oh cool, where's the husband then?

Fuck knows, Joy says, draining her glass.

Erica doesn't respond, just nods.

We need more cocktaaaiiillls, Val sings as she joins them at the table. She summons the waitress and orders three Bruce-Lee-Chinis, a deliciously sickly concoction of vodka, lychee and rose water.

So, what're we talking about? Good old catch up?

Joy was just saying that they've got a carer for some evenings when they're both out, for Seb's Mum.

Oh yeah, he told me that the other day. Genius, really. Better than you both being stuck inside all the bloody time. What's the old man up to?

No idea, Joy says. I asked, but he just said he's out with the guys. Could be the pool hall, could be Ibiza, your guess is as good as mine.

Does this carer person look after the dog, too?

Yeh, he's easy though. I would have bought him with me if it was socially acceptable.

He looks so cute in the pictures, I can't wait to meet him, Erica says.

In the small silence that follows, Erica once again curses herself for making such a bold assumption. That she would be invited to Joy's house, no, her *mother-in-law's* house, to meet her dog.

He loves new people, Joy says, sparing her any further social anxiety.

He pulled off one of my false eyelashes the last time I saw him, says Val. He was tiny and had those little needle teeth that puppies are blessed with. Like a very cute but very annoying baby shark on land.

They laugh at this, the tension easing away a little. The waitress brings over their fresh cocktails and some menus, which Erica and Val already know by heart. Joy lets them order a bunch of stuff for them all to share, trusting that whatever they choose will be good.

By the time the food comes out of the kitchen, they are on their third drink.

All this sugar is going to have us twitching by the end of the night.

Wow, Joy, you're such a Mum now.

I don't have kids?

Exactly, that's why it's weird.

Joy pushes Val's arm and beckons the waitress over to order more drinks.

Prosecco, shall we? Joy suggests.

There she is, Val says, fun Joy lives!

The waitress brings over a cold bottle of bubbles and three glasses, Val pours it out for them.

To us, and to noodles.

To us, and to noodles, they repeat after her.

Erica and Joy descend into silence as they tear into the food in front of them. While neither eat meat, they both insist that fish doesn't count, as they divide the pieces of prawn toast evenly between them.

Joy watches as Erica uses her fork to pick up noodles and dip them in hoisin sauce before stuffing too many of them into her mouth. Erica notices her watching.

Sorry, I'm starving.

Don't say sorry, Joy says, I forgot how much you enjoy food.

The pair laugh, Val watching with a smile on her face, picking at the papaya salad in front of her.

Joy grips some noodles with her chopsticks, then puts them down. Picks up her fork and follows Erica's lead. She scoops up fried rice with a prawn cracker and drizzles it in sweet chilli sauce, puts the whole thing in her mouth. She rolls her eyes back dramatically and lets out a moan.

Bloody hell, it's so much better when you eat like nobody is watching.

I was wondering how long you were going to last with that polite chop stick routine, Erica said.

Been a while since I've been around people that don't find it *uncouth.*

Erica laughs, deposits a piece of prawn toast onto Joy's plate from hers.

A gift, she says, eyes shining.

I'm stuffed, Val says.

Not too stuffed for cheese and wine, I hope.

Don't worry, babes, I'd never do that to you.

They finish off the prosecco and pay the bill, tipping heavily.

The next destination a mere twenty feet away, so they linger outside of the place for a cigarette. Erica offers one to both of them, Joy takes one, Val does not.

Are you never tempted? Erica asks her.

Literally all the time. It's just not worth it in public, somebody could see.

You're not Scarlett Johannsson, Val, the paparazzi aren't following your every move.

I know that, she quips. It's just as bad though, people with camera phones and social media, you know as well as I do that one shitty move on my part could bring everything down.

Fucking sucks, that does. Erica takes a long drag on her cigarette, grateful to always live in the shadows of others, happy that nobody pays her enough notice to give a shit whether she smokes or not.

I'm risking it enough being in a place that serves cheese boards.

Ah yes, Joy says, Miss Vegan Extraordinaire.

I'm only human, Val says. And Petit Café is quiet enough for me to nibble some brie. Also, we'll be the youngest people there, old people don't have Instagram *or* know who I am, so win-win.

Erica feels a pang of sympathy for Val, as she often does when she discusses her job. Clearly made miserable by it, constantly acting, always keeping up appearances. The fact that Val's entire career could be dismantled, or she could be *cancelled* for eating dairy or smoking a cigarette, or doing anything else of the sort, seems wild to Erica. Any weight she gains comes under scrutiny, any that she loses is celebrated. A way to ensure that you are living in a constant state of anxiety.

Val shivers with a breeze and pulls her furry coat around herself.

Sod you two, she says, I'll see you in there.

Erica and Joy watch her totter over the pedestrian crossing, narrowly avoiding being hit as she goes. They watch her stick a finger up to the driver, evidently having drank enough to not care what his particular opinion of her is. She disappears into their next destination, no doubt securing the nicest table.

She doesn't change, does she, Joy says with a smile as she drags on her cigarette.

Nope, thankfully. Wouldn't want her to.

Same. I'm so glad you two ended up being mates here, what a small world.

Yeah, she's lovely.

Joy gives Erica a look.

Lovely? She raises her eyebrows.

Don't be daft, I'm not in *love* with the girl. She lightly punches Joy's arm. My heart is already taken, thank you very much.

They laugh together and stub their cigarettes into an ashtray.

With Frankie, I mean.

Oh, I know.

Right.

The silence threatens to linger, when it is interrupted by the shrill beeping of the pedestrian crossing, and elderly lady next to them having pushed the button.

Come on, Joy says, and links her arm into Erica's.

The immediate thrill that shoots through Erica's body does not shock her at all, she finds it comforting, the inevitability of her longing. The confirmation of her feelings. She focuses on putting one foot in front of the other as they cross the road, ensuring that she doesn't make a fool of herself, or force Joy to let go before she has to. Through the window in front of them, they can see Val waving and pointing at the table she is sat at, as though her being sat at it doesn't indicate that it is theirs. Erica feels a sudden rush of affection for her, her unlikely friend who has made such an effort to bring them together tonight, to make sure they are both comfortable.

Joy lets go of Erica's arm as they reach the doorway to Petit Café, she feels the loss intensely and immediately. The door is opened for them by the waiter, always impeccably dressed and friendly. Erica and Val have spent many nights in here banging the world to rights, he must have overheard so much embarrassing crap over the years.

He nods a hello and shows them to their table which is tucked away in the back corner booth. They step around the jazz band setting up at the front and shuffle onto their seats. Erica watches as Joy takes in her surroundings. Candles lighting the tables, a handwritten wine menu on the wall, two bar staff mixing up long cocktails. Val smacks her on the knee under the table.

Stop staring, she mouths.

Erica blushes immediately, grateful for the dim lighting, hopes it will disguise it.

This place is so cute, Joy says. Anywhere like this in London is always crazy expensive.

I can't believe you're a southerner now, Erica says.

Oh, come on, that's mean, Joy says. If anything, I'm like, a northerner on safari.

The trio laugh, a booze induced easiness settling over them. They order a bottle of wine and a cheese board, and watch as the jazz band finish setting up at the front of the bar.

You guys reckon I'm posh, Joy says, yet you're the ones that have a local that plays live jazz and serves fancy French wines.

Well, we have an excuse, one of us is a celebrity, Erica says, making jazz hands around Val.

Shut it, Val says as she gets up to use the bathroom.

They watch her stumble over the table next to them and stifle their laughter. She would be embarrassed if she knew they'd seen. Erica watches as Val enters the bathroom, hopes that she's stopped her old after-dinner habit. She picks a roasted peanut out of the bowl sat in between them.

That's so gross, I can't believe you still do that, Joy says, horror on her face.

Do what? They're free snacks, Erica says as she pops another into her mouth.

It's full of other people's pee germs, and fuck knows what else.

Come on, it's a nice place, there's probably, like, two peoples pee germs in this bowl, max. You've gotta learn to live on the edge, Erica says with a wink as she chews on another.

So, Joy says, where's Frankie tonight?

Erica recoils internally at having to speak about her to Joy.

Out with the girls.

Nice, same as you then.

Yeah. Not sure she used to shag any of the girls she's out with though.

Joy spills the wine that she is pouring.

Fucking hell, E, give me some warning next time, Joy mops up the spillage and catches her breath. Can you believe that this is what we deem as an acceptable price for wine now? She says, to change the subject.

I imagine you drink a lot pricier stuff than this down in London, no?

Joy shrugs and makes sure there is an equal amount in all three glasses.

Sure, I just mean, like, we used to sit on your mum's garage roof and drink three quid bottles of piss from the corner shop, and now we're here.

God, yeah, remember that stuff? Like necking vinegar.

The pair pull a face and giggle as they clink their glasses and take a sip.

Definitely upgraded, didn't we? Says Joy.

Erica's smile falters. She meant the wine, and Erica knows that, but something in the eye contact between them is making her think in subtexts.

Val returns to the table and grabs her wine glass by the stem.

Right then, to all being together since we were kids down in Brighton. May we continue to get hotter and happier, cheers.

They clink their glasses together and drink, letting the alcohol warm them from the inside out.

They relax into their seats as the lights dim and the band begins to play. Joy turns to Val and mimes that they sound great, a smile stretched across her face. Erica watches Joy as she takes in the music. Her jaw moves slightly as she nibbles on a cracker, totally engrossed in the band.

Erica is transported back to when they were together at a pub gig years ago, some band that was playing Pixies covers. She remembers that same look on Joy's face, wonderment mixed with awe, the reflections of the lights dancing in her eyes, as they are now.

Erica feels a hand on her knee, Val.

Are you okay? She mouths.

Erica nods, shoves a cracker with a wedge of strong blue cheese on top into her mouth.

They stay politely silent while the three piece finishes their few songs, only turning back to the table when the band take a break.

Wow, Joy says, I love them.

First time hearing live jazz, babes?

Yeah, I think so, I love it.

Awh, Erica, we took Joy's jazz virginity.

Erica blushes slightly as they all laugh together.

The waiter comes over to take the remains of the cheese board away, when Val's phone starts vibrating on the table. She snatches it from in front of herself before the name on the screen is visible, and holds up a finger to the girls as she leaves the table to take the call.

Must be Sky News wanting an update on how her weekend is going, Erica says.

Joy hits her arm gently, tells her to stop being so mean.

Val rushes back to their table and grabs her coat from the booth.

Babes, I'm sorry, I have to leave. Totally forgot I'm supposed to be at my friends' party this evening, what a klutz.

You have other *friends*? Erica feigns shock and pretends to faint.

Piss off, they're cooler than you.

She kisses Erica on the cheek and pulls Joy in for a hug.

Love you both, be good. She throws down some cash on the table for her drink and leaves with a wink, coat flung over her shoulder. A taxi stops outside as soon as she lifts her elegant hand into the air.

Well, nice to see Hurricane Valencia, as always.

Joy's phone buzzes, a text from Seb.

Back later than I thought, don't wait up x

Irritation surges through her. She resists the urge to type back something petulant, something that might make him jealous, just for the fun of it. Decides to ignore it all together.

Right, she says. Another drink?

Erica nods, startled.

Good. Not here though. Let's go somewhere fun. Let's go somewhere where there's dancing.

Erm, okay, Erica laughs.

They pay the bill and pull their coats on, adrenaline surging through them.

Joy links her arm through Erica's.

Lead the way, she says, as they walk into the crowded October night.

15

2014 / BRIGHTON

Joy tipped the remains of a nearby bottle of prosecco into a mug and drained it, flopped back onto her pillow. She heard Meg emerge from the bathroom, singing along to Merry Christmas Everyone as it played for what seemed like the tenth time on the radio.

Merry Christmas, baaaaabe, Meg sang from the hallway. Have you decided what you're wearing today?

Joy groaned as she pulled herself up, the hangover subsiding slightly with the addition of new alcohol to her bloodstream.

This, she shouted, holding up a black skater style dress. Meg peered around the doorway to look at it, her hair wrapped in an intricate mess of towels.

Nice, she said, classic. She gave Joy a thumbs up and disappeared into her own room.

Joy checked her phone, nothing new from Seb yet. Not that she was expecting to be the first thought in his mind on Christmas morning when he was home with his family in Liverpool. He had left the day before Christmas Eve; he and Val made the journey together by train. They could both afford first class tickets and were headed to the same posh town. Joy had pretended not to be envious. She missed them both, but was grateful for Meg. Christmas with Meg's family would be nice, and it was a damn sight better than what would have been waiting for her had she joined Val and Seb back to Liverpool. She made a mental note to call her dad at some point, apologise for not being there. She would have to make the call soon, as he always started on the top shelf early on holidays.

She shot a Merry Xmas message to a few friends from her uni course, scrolled through Facebook to see what everyone was up to. The posts were nauseating. The classic and expected engagement posts with tacky looking rings. Huge present piles for one year old kids, posts about the huge presents for one year old kids being used to show off and belittle those less fortunate. The few people from art college who worked at homeless shelters making sure everyone knew about it, selfies with the underprivileged.

Out of habit, she checked Erica's profile. She hadn't updated it in the last year, aside from a picture of her doing her first tattoo at a studio back home that she'd landed an apprenticeship at. Joy studied the picture for the thousandth time, had memorised every pixel of it. Joy tried to push down the bitterness that Erica might be doing okay without her. Maybe she could text her. She rolled the idea round in her head, when her stomach dropped. A new post had been made two days ago.

A picture of Erica, her orange hair tied up in a bun, her face painted like a reindeer. More tattoos than the last time Joy saw her. Pressed against her face, a girl that Joy didn't recognise. Short blonde hair, paint splattered dungarees, with a fake Santa beard on. They were both mid-laugh, mouths open and finding something hilarious. The caption read 'All I want for xmas is you, Santa Baby!'

Joy read it over and over again. A girl. Another girl. Erica had met another girl and was spending a major holiday with her, and this girl was so super-awesome-special that she was all Erica wanted for Christmas. The rational voice in her head told her that it didn't matter, that she had been dating Seb for a month now and they were doing good, why shouldn't Erica have moved on too?

Another voice inside of her was letting out one huge existential scream.

It had been somewhat easy for her to pretend that Erica wasn't real outside of her life, that she had gone back to Liverpool and had ceased to exist on this mortal plane. She never updated her social media, she never got in touch, Joy could almost pretend that the relationship had never happened. But now, faced with the reality of her ex moving on, something ugly bubbled inside of her and was trying to get out. She hated this. Wanted to call her immediately and ask what she thought she was playing at. Wasn't she still heartbroken? Wasn't she missing Joy? Didn't this girl remind her of everything that they had together that she couldn't possibly find again?

Joy chewed at the skin around her fingernails. Meg appeared in the doorway again, her pink hair now dropping down in elegant curls.

You're not even showered? Come on babe, I told Mum we'd be there by twelve to help with peeling and all that shit.

Sorry, Joy mumbled and shoved her phone under her pillow where it could cause no further harm. She threw the duvet back and dragged herself to the bathroom, stepping over two piles of soaking wet towels that Meg had left on the floor. She turned the temperature of the water to its max, but the heat did nothing to clear her mind of the fog that had descended upon it. Somebody else.

As she pulled conditioner through her hair, she wondered if Erica ever checked up on her via social media. If she ever combed through pictures of nights out studied Joy's face, tried to fit the face she was looking at into the memories that she had of her. Maybe Erica was waiting for a reaction from Joy. Maybe she wants her to get in touch? Or maybe she wanted to hurt her with it. Too many possibilities ran through her mind.

When she stepped out the shower, she heard her phone ping from the bedroom. Could it be her? Had she realised what a terrible mistake she had made by leaving? Maybe this new girlfriend had forced her to realise how great they were together.

Joy threw her damp naked body onto her bed and dug the phone out from under the pillow. Seb.

Merry xmas, beautiful. Last night's party here went late, sorry for not texting sooner. Busy today, gotta make sure mum doesn't do a hangover sick in the food! Enjoy Megs place, talk to you later x

She realised she had been holding her breath, and let it go. Tried to ignore the swell of disappointment inside of her.

Merry xmas. Glad the party went well, can't wait to see you x

As she sent the text, she realised she mostly meant it. Why should she stay stuck in the past? Erica had clearly moved on, didn't give a shit about her anymore. She switched over to Facebook and did the ultimate putting-yourself-out-there thing. She changed her Facebook relationship status to 'in a relationship' and sent the request to Seb.

She chewed the skin on her fingers once more. Maybe she should have given him a heads up first. What if he didn't want to display it to the world? It had only been a month, after all. She looked at Erica's post again. Fuck it, she thought. If Erica was going to shove her happiness in everyone's face, then so was she.

She threw her dress on and dried her hair, painted on her usual thick eyeliner and pulled on a pair of boots. She felt strong, like something was about to change. As she stood up quickly, the blood rushed to her head, reminding her that she was still hungover. She sat down again.

Meg, she shouted.

Yeah babe?

What've we got to drink? It's not Christmas morning without booze.

Thought I'd never hear you say those words.

Joy heard Meg rustling round in their kitchen before appearing in the doorway holding two cans of cider.

They clinked them together and took a deep gulp.

I needed that, said Joy.

Come on, Mum's waiting. We can pick up some more drinks on the way.

Joy grabbed her big coat and they set off into the Brighton chill. Arm in arm, laughing all the way.

*

The meal that Meg's mum had cooked was unimaginably huge. She had piled the food in mismatched dishes along the driftwood dining table, allowing people to help themselves. There were ten people in attendance, some being Meg's family, others her Mum's eccentric collection of friends. Joy had spent the afternoon talking with artists, a sculptor, and a woman who made a career out of building birdhouses. The affection in the room was tangible. Meg's mum talked about her daughter proudly, having her explain her recent university projects from start to finish every time one of the others enquired. Joy smiled as she watched, wondering if her mother might have been that way, had she ever met her.

The wine flowed freely all day, the conversations slowly becoming more slurred and sentimental. Meg's mum instructed everyone to pull a record out of her collection and pile them up ready to be played, she held the hand of a friend and twirled around the living room to Fleetwood Mac.

Joy slipped out of the room as the sun was setting. She sat, full of nut roast and potatoes, and smoked a cigarette on the back step. She watched the seagulls soar through the sky, a deep, crisp blue. She pulled her coat around herself, tried to remember the last time she had seen snow on Christmas Day. Must have been when she was a child.

She pulled out her phone and dialled Seb as she blew smoke into the cold air. It rang out, as she expected. Six in the evening, he was most likely sitting around a big table with his family, phone not allowed at the table or something. She dialled Val instead, who picked up. She always picked up.

Babes, hey.

Hey! How's your day going? Is it nice being back with the family?

Oh, yeah, great. It's been fine, yeah. How're you? How's Meg?

Great actually. Her mum's house is really cool, we're all just drinking nice wine and chilling out now. I'm missing you guys! Have you seen Seb since you got there?

Oh, yeah. We had that awful party last night thanks to our parents having friends in common. We've all ended up here again tonight, too.

At least you've had a friend there then! Was it fun? Are you having a good day?

Yeah, fun. I'm sorry babes, I've gotta go, we're doing charades and it's my turn. Love you.

Val hung up before Joy had a chance to respond. She stubbed her cigarette out on the bottom of her boot and threw the end into a nearby plant pot. She thought Val had sounded strained, stressed out. She thought about how she must sound when she is around her dad and put it down to that. Family is enough to stress anyone out.

You okay, love?

Meg's mum appeared in the doorway and offered Joy a fresh cigarette, sat herself down next to her on the step.

Yeah, all good. Thank you so much for having me today.

Always welcome, love. Was that a boy on the phone then?

Oh, no, Joy laughed. He didn't answer, that was our other flatmate, Val.

Ah yes, the leggy one. Where is she today?

Back home in Liverpool, she travelled back with the guy I'm seeing, they both come from the same posh little area.

Hm.

What?

Nothing.

No, seriously, what?

Well, maybe it's just an age thing. I've met that friend of yours, could melt a man from across the room, no? Brave of you to trust your fella around her.

Joy laughed, choked a little on smoke.

It's not like that. Val wouldn't do anything like that.

Well, that's nice, love. What about this lad of yours?

Joy shuffled on the step.

I'd like to think he wouldn't either.

Meg's mum nodded, changed the conversation to the chickens she kept at the bottom of the garden. Apparently, a local fox had taken to visiting at night, so she had been forced to upgrade the security fence to keep them safe from predators.

Meg popped her head around the doorway.

Mum, stop boring Joy to death with fox drama.

She poked at her mum with her fluffy-socked-foot.

Come on, Joy, my fave album is on, and I've cracked open a bottle of some good stuff.

Meg held out a hand and pulled Joy up from the step.

They returned to the front room; full glasses of wine they couldn't appreciate thrust into their hands as they twirled each other around to the song bursting from the speakers of the record player.

For one moment, Joy wasn't thinking of Erica at all.

*

Val sat on the garden chair in front of him, chewing on her fingernails. She had noticed the shift in dynamic on their train journey to Liverpool, thrust together that day after only one brief previous encounter. She had tried to ignore it, failed miserably.

She won't find out, Seb said as he took the seat next to her.

She shivered, he offered his jacket, but she looked at him as though she would be more likely to throw up on it than wear it.

Her finding out isn't what's killing me, it's the fact that it even fucking happened. She's my best mate, we live together. Fuck. I have to tell her.

Seb reached out a hand to put on her shoulder, but she flinched away from him.

I think it's best if we never touch again, don't you? Or even speak to each other.

We can't do that; she will get suspicious. We were fine before, we have to stay that way, otherwise she'll know something happened.

She'll know something happened because I'm going to fucking tell her, Seb.

No, you're not.

Val scoffed.

What, can't face up to the consequences of your actions?

She looked at him with venom in her eyes.

They were your actions too, Val. What, you think she's going to forgive you because you come clean? Yeah right. She'll be angry. Hurt. Devastated that her best friend could do that to her. She'll kick you out or move out herself. You'll probably never see her again.

Seb, I can't just go back to Brighton and pretend nothing happened!

Well, you have to. I'm sorry but you have no choice. This affects me too. I don't want to lose her.

Shouldn't have fucked her best mate then, should you?

Come on, you know there was this… heat, between us. I think we both knew that this was going to happen.

What?

Val, don't act dumb. Despite what people think about you, I know you're not.

Val felt a lunge in her stomach, a twist of the knife that she had put there herself. She held on tightly to her thighs.

You're Joy's boyfriend, she said weakly.

And I'm going to stay that way. It would never work out, me and you, you're too… I don't know, independent?

Is that supposed to be an insult?

No, just– look, you and Joy, you're very different people. She's the opposite of the girls I normally go out with, she's–

I get it, no need to continue. I'm not into you, Seb, this was just a stupid drunken mistake.

Keep telling yourself that.

Val shuffled in her seat.

Look, we need to go back to Brighton and be business as usual, neither of us want to lose Joy.

Val looked at her shoes, kicked a stray pebble with her toe.

Val, Seb said, sternly.

He stood up and lifted her chin with his thumb and finger.

She can never know. I need to know that you understand that.

Tears filled her eyes. Always a terrible liar, how would she ever keep hold of this secret? How would she be able to live with what she had done to a person she loved so much?

Seb repeated her name, not letting go of her chin.

Fine, she said in a small voice.

Pardon?

I said fine.

Good. Now, let's go and get this horrendous charade out of the way.

He pointed towards the living room, where their two families were in fact, playing charades. He smirked at her. She hated herself for the longing she could feel within her, the undeniable attraction she felt to this man.

Val let the tears come.

I'll be in in a moment.

Cool, I'll pour you a drink. Champagne?

Val nodded, watched as Seb slipped back into his stage persona as he entered the kitchen and slapped her dad on the back, pulled him a beer out of the fridge, made the room laugh heartily with some anecdote or another. She saw him look at his phone and pocket it again.

Seconds later, her phone rang in her pocket, Joy. Fuck. She answered, tried to keep her replies short and sweet, told her she had to go, that it was her turn in charades. Seb met her eyes from inside the house, she did a thumbs up and wiped her face dry with the sleeve of her Balenciaga jumper. Deep breath.

Her Mum beckoned from inside for her to join them, she motioned that she would be two minutes, made her way to the downstairs bathroom.

What sort of bitch was she turning into, to be able to do this kind of thing and keep it to herself? To let herself give in to a stupid crush on the most inappropriate man she could have found. Self-loathing flowed through her, she felt disgusted with herself. She locked the bathroom door, avoided the mirror and dropped to her knees, before quietly, expertly, releasing her dinner into the toilet.

*

Joy had awaited their return on the twenty eighth of December eagerly. Since Christmas at Meg's mum's house, the pair had returned to their flat and done little other than eat chocolates and watch festive movies under a blanket. That strange liminal space between Christmas Day and New Years where airport rules reigned and you could drink at any time of the day without judgement.

Joy had gotten up early that morning, opened the living room curtains for the first time in just under a week. She grabbed a bin bag and piled the debris of the festive period into it; empty cans, chocolate boxes, takeout bags, cigarette butts. She opened the windows and lit candles, wiped down the surfaces and hoovered the carpets. Their ancient Henry Hoover spluttered out sounds of pure shock as she plugged it in and whipped it round their flat. She put new sheets on her stale bed, threw all of her clothes into the washing machine.

When she heard the taxi door slam outside of their building, her heart was in her throat. She realised her smile probably looked manic, but didn't care, she had missed them both so much.

When the front door opened, she flung her arms around Val first, who hugged her weakly in return.

You're home! I put new sheets on your bed for you, and I got us a fancy bottle of fizzy stuff for later, too.

Ah, she said, thanks babes.

Val walked past her and into her bedroom, closed the door quietly.

Long journey, Seb said from the doorway.

She felt her knees turn to jelly as he smiled at her and held out his arms.

Hey beautiful, how are you?

Better now you're here, she said, feeling like a lead in a cliché rom com.

She jumped up and wrapped her legs around his waist as he grabbed her, kissed him firmly on the lips.

I put clean sheets on my bed too, made it all tidy, she said.

Oh, did you? I see. Well. Better go mess it back up then.

He kissed her again and kicked the front door shut with his foot.

She laughed as he carried her to her bedroom, feeling like she was where she was meant to be, and heading straight into her future.

16

2019 / LIVERPOOL

The cold is getting worse, Val thinks as she taps her foot impatiently on the pavement. She already regrets leaving Erica and Joy, hopes they didn't suspect anything. Her stomach groans, aching from the ordeal of eating all that Chinese food and then puking it back up. She should have had some of that cheese board before she left, her mouth waters at the thought of it. She curses her ridiculous job for having to be so secretive about her dairy consumption.

So many lies.

She checks her phone instinctively as soon as she thinks of work, taps on the Instagram notifications, watches them flood in. She flits her eyes up from her screen, scanning the passing crowds for his face. Her heart leaps whenever she thinks she spots him, an unfortunate response to the husband of one's best friend. They have been out a few times since he has returned to Liverpool, Val telling herself that it was as friends, nothing more, but the heat between them is still undeniable.

He knows it, he uses it. She lets him.

She checks her phone again, no message since his last one telling her where to meet him. She lets out an impatient sigh and scrolls through her notifications. Her most recent post was a selfie, promoting a new underwear set from a sustainable underwear company, whatever that is. One thousand and forty-five comments sit underneath it. She clicks on them to look through.

Omgggg hun you look amazing, so jealous!

if I were twenty years younger hahaha

is the packaging this company uses recyclable? If not, u should be ashamed!

Ewwwwww slut

She lets them wash over her, rereads the hurtful ones. Briefly considers throwing her phone into the Mersey and retreating to the woods to live off the grid. Remembers that she hates spiders and that the woods are probably full of them. Some part of her sees reading the nasty comments as penance for her actions, some sort of punishment for her deceit, although a larger part of her knows it would never be enough to pay for what she has done. What she is doing.

As she slips her phone back into her Louboutin bag, he appears in front of her, hair dishevelled from the wind, apologetic smile on his face.

Sorry, sorry, Uber took forever to find me.

She huffs in response, lets him open the door for her as they enter the bar. She takes off her coat and instantly feels the warmth of his hand on the small of her back. Adrenaline floods through her like hot whiskey on a cold day, warming every part of her body.

I was waiting ages, you know. What if the girls had seen?

They're back at the French place, no?

Well, yeah, but they could have left, gone somewhere else, seen me lingering around. Liverpool really isn't that big, Seb.

Calm down, he says in that soothing tone, the one that both relaxes her and annoys the living shit out of her at the same time.

They didn't see, we're here. Let's grab a table, drinks are on me.

She smiles, despite herself, lets a pretty, brunette waitress with a nametag that says Lauren show them to a table in the corner.

So, how was it, the night out?

Oh, really nice. Food is always great from there, and the jazz band was on in Petit Café.

Mmh, not my thing, but I'm glad you had fun. How many wines deep was Joy when you left?

I wasn't aware I was supposed to be counting.

An impossible task, in my experience.

You're strangely bothered about your wife's alcohol consumption for a man that is out on a date with another woman right now.

What's that got to do with it?

Just… I don't know. Just don't act like you have some sort of moral high ground over Joy, you most definitely don't.

Point taken.

He reaches across the table for her hand, but she pulls it away.

Come on, Seb, you know that's not cool, not while we're out.

A cackle erupts from the far corner of the bar, a group of pissed-up women that Val clocked on their way in. She didn't look their way, didn't want to draw attention to her presence.

Lauren returns to take their drinks orders, a pint and a Pornstar martini, their usual. Val pushes down the familiar pang of painful guilt as the waitress leaves their table, probably presuming that they are a happy couple out on a date.

So, he starts.

So.

How's work?

Don't pretend that you think I have a proper job.

I do, of course I do, it's just a bit odd to me that's all. But I totally understand why you get paid to be pretty.

He drops his hand under the table, rests his hand on her knee, the familiar fizzle of excitement hits her immediately.

There's a bit more to it than that.

Oh, yes, of course, of course.

And you? How's work?

Busy, yeah. The London office is crazy at the moment, and the one we have here is getting more attention.

Yeh, I heard. Joy said you've been there quite a lot while you've been back?

He looks at her, questioningly.

What?

That's what I've been telling her when I've been seeing you.

Oh.

Yeah.

Right, of course.

An uncomfortable silence follows as the waitress brings their drinks over, sets them down in front of them.

Val thanks her, but she doesn't leave the table.

I just wanted to ask, you're Valencia, aren't you?

Seb leans back in his chair, hand removed from her knee, amusement on his face.

Yes, I am.

Oh my god, I knew it. Me and all my friends follow you on Instagram, I even went vegan because of you.

Oh, wow, that's so nice, thank you.

Val pastes on the expression that she has perfected over the last few years. Look grateful, look pretty, look humbled all at the same time.

Super cool to meet you, Lauren gushes as she tucks her notepad back into her apron. She glances at Seb and smiles a wide grin before rushing off back to the bar. Val can't help herself but watch the inevitable scene unfold as Lauren returns to her colleagues to tell them, that some woman they've never heard of who is Instagram famous for nothing is in their bar. She watches the indifference on their faces as they shrug, uncaring, not recognising her name. Lauren holds out her phone, presumably showing them her profile. A nod from two of the men, acknowledging that she isn't unattractive, then turning back to their tasks behind the bar.

She hopes that Lauren doesn't take a photo, not while she is with Seb. Since he has come back and they have been meeting up, she has insisted on discreet venues, hotels or her apartment. She is suddenly very aware that they are stupidly sat a five-minute walk from her date's wife.

Wow, Seb starts, looking between Lauren and Val.

Don't.

Don't what?

Just… don't.

Okay, okay, I won't say anything.

Good.

A beat of silence passes between them.

Just didn't realise you were so famous, that's all.

Seb, for fucks sake.

I'm kidding, calm down, that was super cute.

Cute?

Yeah, you have like, actual proper fans, it's adorable.

I'll pretend that that's a compliment.

You should.

She allows a smirk to creep onto her face as he knocks her foot with his under the table.

These are Louboutin's, pal, you mark them you buy me new ones.

Oh, really? Well, I'll have to get you out of them as soon as possible.

He leaves his knee touching hers, returns his hand to her knee, his grip firm.

The raw desire deep in her stomach is suddenly at war with guilt again. Seb must sense it, she thinks, as he regains his composure, sits straighter, brings his feet back under his own chair.

He clears his throat, checks his phone, puts it face down on the table in front of him.

Joy?

What? Oh, no, just making sure there's nothing from Mum.

How is she?

Pain in the arse, but with a broken leg.

Nice. Worth the trip back, then?

We've barely seen her, to be honest. Absolutely pointless us being here, she's got all her cronies running errands, a private care person to tend to her every whim when we're not there, it's silliness.

How come you're sticking around then?

He looks at her pointedly.

Me?

You, V.

She nods, digs her nails into her thigh under the table.

We haven't seen each other in forever, despite my best efforts.

Are you referring to you trying to set me up with that creep you're friends with?

Jason?

Jason, yeah.

I thought it would get you down to ours.

And what if I'd fallen in love with him or something?

Ha, fat chance of that, he is everything you despise. Joy, too.

Right, Val says, the pieces fitting together in her mind.

So, you set me up with him, knowing I'd hate him, and you'd have me there with no competition?

Well, no need to make it sound so gross, but yeah. Plus, no suspicion from Joy if you're there on a date.

It's weird, you both being here together. I feel way more guilty than usual.

I know you do.

Maybe we should stop this, at least until you're back in London?

What? That's crazy, V. Aren't you enjoying the time we have together? No sneaky weekends in weird middle-of-nowhere hotels, no stolen nights midweek; I haven't had to make up a stag do or a conference or any of that cliché bullshit.

I guess.

Come on, you can't make out like I'm forcing you to do this.

I know, I'm not, sorry. It just feels inevitable that someone is going to get hurt.

Here you go, Lauren interrupts, as she returns to their table with drinks.

She sets the drinks down in front of them, Val grabs her glass by the stem and takes two deep gulps, licks the foam from her top lip.

Seb smiles at her in that way that he always has, like she is small, soft, as though she is his to take care of. She blushes under his gaze, always has done. With every sip of her drink, the guilt edges further and further away, until it is nothing but a faint whisper, somewhere deep at the back of her mind.

I don't want anybody to get hurt either, Seb finally replies.

I know.

But I also can't stop this, you can't either, we've tried, haven't we?

We have.

And it didn't work, did it?

Evidently not.

I think it would break my heart if we called it a day now, it's been so long.

Val does a small cough on the sip of martini in her mouth, is not used to Seb being so forthcoming with his feelings.

Don't look so shocked, he says, it's not a secret how I feel about you.

You don't often say it, that's all.

You'd think our long-standing affair would say enough.

She looks at him then, an irritated expression that could almost pass as genuine.

Look, he says, this isn't ideal, it never has been. I wish just as much as you do that, we could go back to that first night, come clean, and this could have been a relationship, not the sordid thing that it's become.

She sips her drink, lets him continue.

But that's not how it has happened, and I can't not see you.

She nods a little, places her manicured hand on his under the table. She drains her glass, pulls the confidence out of thin air.

I think, at least while you're here, this has to stop.

A look of pure hurt passes over his face, he regains his neutral expression as quickly as his brain will allow him to.

Because of her?

I just… I can't do this in front of her, it feels shitty enough when I don't have to live in the same city as her.

He stares into the remainder of his pint, nods slowly.

Fine.

Okay?

Fine, sure.

Seb, please, I'm not doing this to hurt you, it's so that we don't hurt anyone else.

No, no, I get it, I do.

Everything inside of Val is screaming at her, demanding that she take it back, suck her words back in somehow, go back to the delicious tension of ten minutes ago, take him home, let his body melt into hers. She stays strong.

So, when I get back to London?

Let's see how we both feel then, yeah?

Right, yeh, okay.

She half smiles at him, reaches out for his hand again, but he draws it away.

He drains his pint.

I'm going to get home, I think.

No, come on, stay out, let's get another round in, or we could go somewhere else?

V, I can't. I can't just be around you, not when it's just us. Not if you won't let us be… us.

The voice inside of Val is screaming louder than ever. Take it back, take it all back, kiss him, kiss him, *kiss him.*

He stands up, walks to the bar to pay their bill. She watches him, this man that for years she has had inside of her head, inside of her body, in her bed. She watches the familiar way that he opens his jacket pocket, always forgetting that he keeps his wallet in his trouser pocket now, after it got stolen on a weekend, they had in the Lake District together. His jacket had been slung over the back of his chair in a small pub, the fire keeping them warm. An opportunist took it whilst they kissed, an inappropriate kiss for in public, but they never cared when they weren't on home turf. Freedom was rare.

She watches him locate his wallet, pull out some notes, leave extra for the waitress. She thanks him over enthusiastically, smiles too much. Val recognises the expression on her face, bashful in the presence of this overtly handsome man. She feels something akin to jealousy bubble up inside of her, wants to link her arm through his, kiss his stubbled cheek, let everyone know that he belongs to her. Instead, she smiles weakly when he returns to the table, grabs her bag.

Ready to go? I'll get you an Uber.

Oh, thanks, I'm going to walk, though. It'll take longer in a cab getting through town at this time.

You know I can't walk you home, right? If I come to your place, I'm not going to want to leave.

I know, I wasn't hinting.

He looks hurt, but she can't soften the blows, can't relent, she is too close to breaking.

He lifts his arm into the air, hails a black cab that is driving past.

I erm... fuck. V, this is going to be difficult.

I know, I'm sorry.

No, I get it, I get it.

He hugs her awkwardly, she tries not to inhale the familiar smell of his neck, doesn't let herself linger too long, or hold him too tightly.

Bye, then.

See you soon.
Hope so.
With that, he is gone.

Val pulls a cigarette out of her emergency pack, sits on the stone steps of the apartment building next to the bar and lights it up, wipes a tear roughly from her face. This is the right thing, she knows it, the situation completely inevitable. One of them had to make the call one day, difficult as it is. This thing that they have had is not sustainable, not without the suffering of other people, let alone their own.

Val wonders if she loves him, if she would have been doing this all of these years if she didn't. She doesn't let herself ponder that question often, can't bring herself to face the consequences of either answer. Either she is in love with a man she cannot have, not fully, or she is fucking her friend's husband to fill some sad, desperate void inside of herself.

She doesn't want to think about either option, and so drags on her cigarette, watches a group of friends hold onto each other as they drunkenly stumble to the next destination. One shouts that she has a text from her ex, to the boos and jeers of her friends. Val watches them, arm in arm, and thinks of all those times, years ago in Brighton, huddled up with Joy, Meg, their lovely friends, bar to bar, having a blast.

Val feels her body moving before she realises what she is doing. She gets up, throws her cigarette to the ground, and is walking, determinedly, back towards the French bar. She is going to get it all out, tell Joy everything, let her scream, cry, let Joy hit her over and over and over again for what she has done, what she has betrayed. She wants to get it all out, start fresh, be able to tell Seb that it's all over, the lying, that it doesn't have to happen anymore, that they can either be together or never see each other again and it won't matter because nobody else's happiness will be on the line.

She rounds the corner and dodges the traffic, sees the jazz

band playing through the window despite the condensation. She walks past the security guy at the door and searches the faces of the crowd, pushes through to the table they had been sat at. She finds two middle aged men in place of Joy and Erica; the remains of the cheeseboard being cleaned up and taken away by a waitress.

Then, she cries. Concerned looks pass between the men in front of her, she doesn't care. She leaves the bar again, storms down Duke Street in the direction of her flat, brushes hard past the shoulders of drunken passers-by who can't walk straight, shrugs off the concerned voices of boozy students. She digs her fingernails into her thighs, waits for the familiar relief.

Just leave me alone, she thinks, I just need to be alone, I deserve to be alone.

17

2019 / LIVERPOOL

Frankie had seen them come in, was even going to go over and say hello. Something had stopped her, perhaps the way that Val was avoiding eye contact with everyone in the place, or how Seb was resting his hand on her lower back, like she was his. Frankie had slumped back into her chair with her bright pink cocktail, joined in half-heartedly with her friends' drinking game, kept one eye on the situation revealing itself before her.

She knew that Val was supposed to be with Erica and Joy tonight, Val's presence being the only reason that she hadn't insisted on coming, knowing that her girlfriend wouldn't be left alone with the ex. They must be alone now, Frankie thought, her heart felt heavy as she checked her phone to no notifications.

Frankie knew it was Sebastian, recognised him immediately from the hours spent digging through Joy's social media profiles, always keeping one eye on her, always unsure as to exactly why.

She had seen pictures of Joy's home, their dog, their perfect lives in London, tucked away in an affluent suburb. Pictures of their evenings out at fancy restaurants, or pictures that Joy had posted of food she had cooked, crafting dinners for the large parties they hosted for his friends. She remembers looking at those pictures and feeling envious, a green-eyed monster for this woman who did nothing to afford her own lifestyle, who married rich and was reaping the rewards of it, who still had some sort of hold over her girlfriend.

Frankie wonders if Joy knows about this meeting between her

husband and best friend.

Doubts it, by the way they are looking at each other.

Her friends drink and chatter around her, talk of going to a bar with more atmosphere is floating around the table. Frankie nods and mumbles agreement, when necessary, but stays quietly focussed on the scene unfolding before her. Without context, you'd assume they were a couple. Both beautiful, all eye contact and small touches. Perhaps close friends, Frankie thinks. She knows she and her friends are touchy feely all the time. But this seems different.

Seb leans over to say something into Val's ear, Frankie curses her friends internally for being so loud, as if she would have been able to hear the whispered words had they not been cackling at a bad joke.

Where are Erica and Joy?

She gets out her phone, still no notifications from Erica, no point checking her Instagram, she never updates it. She switches to Instagram anyway, and types in Joy's handle, she knows it by heart now, but doesn't follow her. That would make her look crazy.

@JustJoy_

The little pink circle around her profile picture is illuminated, she has posted a story, maybe a few. Maybe it's just loads of boring pictures of her dog. Maybe it's nudes of her and Erica together. She shakes that irrationality away. If she clicks on it, her name will appear on the list of people who have viewed it. Joy will be able to see. If she checks such things, that is. She looks at the profile staring back at her, perfectly curated pictures of a woman, her husband, their dog, some food.

Boring, Frankie thinks. Surely Erica would never harbour feelings for this bland woman on the screen in front of her. But she doesn't want to seem needy, like she's checking up on her, like she's *threatened* by her.

She sucks the remainder of her cocktail through her straw

and decides she doesn't fucking care, clicks on the story, holds her finger to the screen so that it pauses.

A dimly lit bar, not far from here, she recognises it immediately although has never been inside. Lots of candles, tiny lights on strings. In the next story sits the remains of a cheese board, two almost empty glasses of wine behind it. Written on it in small white writing, 'a delicious evening'.

Frankie taps the screen again but there are no more stories posted. Anger bubbles up inside of her small chest. Delicious? The cheese, she hopes, nothing more.

She flicks over to her text messages, types one out to Erica, tries to sound breezy.

Hey babe, having fun? I'm a little tired, might head home soon. Or I could meet you guys? How are Joy and Val? Xo

She knows that she has set herself up for hurt, no matter the response. Already knows that she won't get an invite to join them. The woman that she lives with, the one who has been distracted since her ex's arrival, is finally where she wants to be, with who she wants to be with. She feels it in her gut.

She looks up as Seb and Val get out of their seats, ready to leave. They look sad. She wonders why, but can't muster the energy necessary to make guesses.

Come on, then! Her friends are shouting with glee, eagerly urging those with unfinished drinks to down them.

Where are we going?

Anywhere! Somewhere fun!

Frankie pretends to think for a second.

How about we go to that drag bar at the bottom of Duke Street? Just past that French place?

Oooooh fun!

Yes! Let's go!

The group stand up, a flurry of furry coats and scarves and

excited, half cut voices. They leave the bar and enter the chill of the city, some of them linking arms to stay warm on the short walk to the next bar.

Frankie spots the French bar up ahead, makes sure to steer her friends towards that side of the street so that they can walk past it. She isn't sure what she is expecting to see. Her girlfriend and Joy dry humping on the table? Kissing in front of a crowd of cheering onlookers? She feels ridiculous already, but cannot help herself.

The red man on the crossing finally switches to green and they totter across the road, the sound of their heels on tarmac akin to a pack of light-footed deer trotting together. As they walk past the bar, Frankie turns her head and scans the interior. Old couples, jazz band, tired looking waiter, one girl sat by herself on her phone, a group of friends clinking their glasses together. No sign of Joy or Erica.

She feels herself deflate, jealously, suspicion and hurt seeping out of every pore on her body. Where *are* they? Where the fuck are they?

She feels her eyes get hot, but blinks it back. Her lashes far too expensive of an ordeal to subject them to tears. She links arms with her friends and continues down the road with them, desperately trying not to think about what could be unfolding between the pair right now.

18

2014 / LIVERPOOL

Erica had been lying around the house for weeks waiting for Joy to turn up and apologise. She had ignored every phone call, every text, wanting to push Joy to show her how much she meant to her, that she was worth more to her than those arseholes she'd met in Brighton. Was their relationship not worth the train fare? Could she really not make the journey to fix what she had so casually broken?

The doorbell never sounded. After a few months, as autumn turned into winter, she downloaded Tinder out of curiosity. The healing power of making snap judgements on people, swiping yes or no, was surprising.

The first date that she went on was a total disaster. The girl, Rose, had described herself as '22, exploring, love to travel'. Erica waited at Salt Dog Slims, the agreed upon bar, sipping a delicious yet overpriced cocktail, pushing away thoughts of Joy as she prepared herself to meet a prospective new girlfriend.

She needn't have worried. Rose turned up with her tracksuit clad boyfriend on her arm. They both sat down opposite a dumfounded Erica, all nervous smiles and polite hellos. The look of shock on Erica's face must have been obvious, as Rose promptly explained that the word 'exploring' on her profile was referring to she and her boyfriend looking for a third.

Erica excused herself to the bathroom and made a run for it.

The second had been more successful. A beautiful psychology student named Susie, with wide eyes and freckled shoulders. They had two drinks in an old man pub, then promptly went back to Susie's student house and had sex for the rest of the evening, only interrupted by cigarette breaks and a few hours' sleep.

Erica had left early the next morning when Susie woke her and informed her that she had a lecture to get to. Erica had leaned in for a kiss upon leaving, but the door was quickly closed, leaving Erica with nothing but a taxi waiting, and the taste of her still in her mouth. After several ignored text messages, Erica gave up, accepted that she had been used as a one-night stand. She spent the following week in bed, scrolling through Joy's social media posts. A man had been featuring heavily in them lately, his body pressed against Joy's, his arm around Valencia's tiny waist, she didn't want to know more about him.

She made herself come to the memory of the last time she and Joy had had sex right where she lay, and went to sleep alone.

19

2019 / LIVERPOOL

Joy and Erica land on a tequila bar that resembles a public toilet, tucked down a side street that smells like one. Coats come off immediately, the immense heat of the small space packed with sweating bodies hitting them like it does when you exit a plane in a foreign country.

They fight their way to the bar, order three shots each in different flavours, whatever the bartender had recommended to them. The playlist; mid 2000's pop punk. After slamming four tequilas each, Joy and Erica make their way through the five deep bar crowd to the small area reserved for dancing. They cling to each other, laughing between dance moves, letting the rhythm guitars that narrated their teenage years flow through their bodies. Surrounded by students, sweating and intoxicated, they raise their arms and sway, screaming out the lyrics of their old favourite songs into each other's faces.

In the toilets, Erica checks her phone, texts from Frankie, she can tell how much her girlfriend has tried to disguise her rising panic at the lack of replies.

She sits on the loo and wipes the sweat from her brow, holds her thumping head in her hand as she types out a reply with the other. When she exits the graffitied stall, Joy is waiting for her, a smile stretched across her porcelain face.

I need to leave, Erica shouts above the music and muddled voices of Bathroom Girls giving each other pep talks.

What? Now?

Yeh, sorry, it's Frankie, I-

She lifts her phone screen to Joy so she can see what is going on, whose face falls immediately. She nods, gestures that they should leave the bathroom.

The atmosphere has changed, the crowd that they were just a part of now seems sticky, annoying, too dense to get through. They push their way to the door, stepping on feet and trying not to get drinks spilt on them, an anonymous hand aggressively squeezes Joy's behind as they go. She doesn't bother trying to figure out who it was.

The bar spits them out into the cold night, they both pull on their coats start walking.

You'll have a nightmare getting a cab from here you know.

Erica gestures at the crowded street, music blaring from every door, people sitting in the gutters with their heads lolling as their friends try to feed them water.

Fuck, didn't think of this bit.

Walk to mine, an Uber will get you from there.

Joy looks at the line waiting for black cabs, girls in short dresses sharing a bag of chips, a group of pink men in tight trousers arguing loudly over somebody called Helen. She nods, links her arm through Erica's and they walk towards the quiet.

Once they leave the chaos of the crowds, Joy lets out a big exhale.

It's a lot, isn't it.

Town? God, yeah, I'd forgotten, I think. Too many people.

Definitely. Glad we went, though.

Me too. How far is your place?

Erica points at a building on a corner a few streets away in front of them. Joy follows her finger, sees a brick apartment building around five floors high, the balconies lit up and decorated in different ways.

One of those yours?

Nah, other side of the building, facing the cathedral, it's dead pretty at night.

I bet.

I'd ask you up, honestly, it's just, Frankie, I think, I don't know, probably for the best if you don't.

Yeah, no, I get it. We should do something all together, Joy says, a small tequila flavoured burp following her words.

For sure, that'd be great.

This weekend then, let's do it, I'll cook.

Yeah? Seb's Mum won't mind?

Joy shrugs her shoulders as they reach the door to the apartment building, the street dimly lit with one working lamppost. She pulls out her crumpled pack of cigarettes, places one between Erica's lips, one between her own.

Light?

Here.

The smiley faced lighter is passed between them, neither of them acknowledging what it is, when it is from, why it is still in their possession. Too big of a piece of nostalgia for what they used to be.

They lean against the bare bricks, blowing smoke into the cold air. Joy considers talking, telling Erica that she isn't ready for the evening to end yet. Tries to think of something to say that could prolong this moment, just the two of them, expand it, live inside of it, hold it tightly.

I owe you so many cigs, Erica says.

I've been keeping count, don't you worry.

Erica leans into her playfully, lingers there for a second longer than necessary.

Joy gains the courage to turn her head, to look into her eyes. Still as astonishing at that first meeting in the college smoking shelter.

Still, no words come, just the look between them saying enough.

Erica's phone vibrates against her thigh, shocking her to stand straight, Joy feels the absence of her immediately, viscerally.

It's Frankie, she says.

Joy nods.

Go on, I'll order an Uber from down here.

I can wait?

It's okay, honestly. See you very soon, I'll text you the details. Thanks for tonight.

Thank you, too.

A hug then, tight but fleeting.

Joy watches as Erica turns and swipes her fob on the door, closes it softly behind her. She watches as Erica pushes the button on the lift and lets her hair down out of its bun, a river of colour. Erica turns with a small wave, and disappears behind the lift doors.

Joy lets out a long, deep sigh before getting out her phone to book a cab, texts Seb to let him know she won't be long, that they need to chat about the weekend.

Time to plan a dinner.

20

2019 / LIVERPOOL

The doorbell rings twenty minutes earlier than they had agreed, sending Joy into an immediate panic. It's not ready yet, it won't be ready for a while longer, she hates cooking whilst people watch. She gets sweaty. Sweaty isn't what you want your host to be. Seb notices her floundering and gets up from his seat at the kitchen island.

I'll get it, stop panicking.

He strides out of the kitchen, followed by a cloud of his favourite aftershave.

She is grateful. Quickly darts an eye over at her mother-in-law, who has strategically placed her wheelchair in a position that has allowed her to observe every move Joy has made in the kitchen. Occasionally she tuts, or mutters that she wouldn't have done the potatoes that way.

Joy regains focus, throws the stuffing into the oven and runs her fingers through her hair. She had been happy with her appearance earlier in the morning, chose an all-black outfit and carefully applied red lipstick, styled her hair into a perfect sleek bob. She catches her eye in the reflective back splash and wants to cry at her current state of dishevelment.

She hears Seb's voice booming greetings from the hallway. They're here. It had taken some convincing to get him to agree to today. A booze fuelled invite on the night out with Erica, several texts filled with the promise of her famous roast dinner, because she simply *must* meet Frankie properly, and *of course* Seb will love having the two of you over, and don't be *silly*, Margaret won't mind at *all*.

Seb gave in when Val invited herself, relenting as he has barely seen her while they've been back. Joy admires their friendship, often wonders if he knows how many men would pay to have Val over to their home for dinner.

Val arrives into the kitchen in her usual glamourous manner, oversized faux fur coat and perfect makeup, her hair swept into one of those annoyingly casual looking buns that must take ages to do.

Babes, she sings, it smells insane in here.

Thanks, Joy says quietly, never knowing quite how to take praise.

Val envelopes her in a hug, which, given the coat, feels like hugging the Cookie Monster. Bernie emerges from the living room to greet her, Val scratches his head with her long, decorated nails.

Hey boy, how are you? He licks her hand, which she politely pretends she doesn't mind.

And Margaret, she wipes her hand on her coat and turns around. You poor angel, how are you feeling?

I'm grand, love, on the mend every day.

Margaret pulls her perfect woe is me face which she works on daily, as Val bends down to kiss her on the cheek.

It's lovely to see you, how long must it have been?

Val strokes her chin and thinks back.

Years, she lands on.

Years, yes. Probably at one of those ghastly Christmas parties your parents and I used to drag you both to.

Joy busies herself with stirring a bechamel sauce for her cauliflower cheese, gives Bernie a piece of carrot that he has been eyeing up. She vaguely remembers them returning from one of those Christmas parties. The atmosphere strange and heavy, the details never disclosed.

Seb interrupts and asks who needs a drink, they both request prosecco. As he pours, the doorbell rings again. Bernie runs to greet them.

Remind me, Margaret says to Val, who is this again?

Our old friend and her *partner*.

Ah, yes, the partner.

Joy shuffles uncomfortably, tries to ignore the implication in the tone of that comment. She takes a deep breath and arranges herself in a way that conveys she is concentrating on the cauliflower cheese assembly; but is also sexy and cool whilst doing so. Is that possible? She hopes so.

She hears Seb shoo the dog away and introduce himself, always the charmer in social situations, even ones he doesn't necessarily want to be in. The sound of heels click-clacking on the tile gets louder as Frankie enters the kitchen, a pastel pink vision that could have come straight out of a Barbie box.

Her blonde curls bounce on her shoulders as she hugs Val and introduces herself to Margaret, her high-pitched voice punctuated with a dazzling smile. Margaret looks perplexed, this is definitely not who she was expecting to walk through the door.

Erica enters behind her, Joy's double in all black and tight jeans, with the addition of her trademark flannel shirt, buttoned to her neck. Her orange hair is piled on top of her head, the Primark version of what Val's hair looks like. She sits on the floor immediately and ruffles Bernie's fur, lets him lick her face.

It's so nice to finally meet you, sir. She holds out a hand as she formally greets the dog, he gives his paw in return.

Joy can't help but stare at them, a giddy smile on her face.

Erica releases herself from Bernie's love and heads straight to Joy. They hug tightly, any awkwardness between them long gone.

This all looks so good, I can't fucking *wait* to shovel potatoes into my face.

Margaret clears her throat from across the room, disapproving of the language.

Ah, you must be Seb's Mum.

Erica walks over and leans down to hug her, but is met by Margaret's outstretched hand. She shakes it, not bothering to mask her amusement, and turns back to Joy.

So, what's on the menu? I am staaaarrrrving.

You won't be for long; you know I have no sense of portion control. Joy laughs as she pours the bechamel sauce over the cauliflower and puts it into the oven to join everything else. She wipes her forehead with a tea towel.

Do you need a drink? Erica asks.

Absolutely.

Joy looks over at the others, Seb has poured them all Proseccos and is opening the bi folding doors out to the garden. It is one of those glorious days in October when the sun is shining, but the ground is frosty. He ushers them into the garden where they have a heated seating area. Frankie and Val hang on to each-other to make it over the grass in heels. Seb steers his Mum's wheelchair, quick glances over at Val to make sure she doesn't fall in her shoes.

The relief as they leave the house is palpable, too many people in the kitchen makes her nervous. She pulls a bottle of wine out of the fridge and finds two glasses, pours them both a large.

You really fucking hate hosting, don't you? Erica laughs as they clink glasses.

I'm honestly not sure at this point. It is simultaneously great and terrible.

She takes a deep gulp of her wine and checks the timer on her phone, an hour until the food is ready. An hour of entertaining people.

You definitely hate it, Erica says, observing her.

Shut up, Joy nudges her arm. Let's go and save your poor girlfriend from the wrath of my mother-in-law.

They walk over the lawn to the seating area, Seb has lit the chiminea and is talking quietly to Val, his attention focused solely on her. She laughs at something he says. He always makes her laugh. Frankie and Margaret appear deep in conversation, Margaret feeling Frankie's hair in her fingers. Joy can hear her listing the names of different places she buys her extensions from. She glances at Erica, who looks equally perplexed that everyone is getting on so well.

Bernie bounds out of the house with a tennis ball in his mouth, he takes it over to the group to see who might like to throw it for him. He avoids Margaret, experience from their time here has taught him quickly that she most definitely will not play with him. He nudges Seb, but he shoos him away, he and Val deep in quiet conversation. She watches them for a moment, the looks on their faces, there is such familiarity between them.

She is distracted when Bernie drops the ball on Frankie's lap, and backs away as she lets out a high-pitched squeal. She picks up the ball with the tips of her nails and drops it on the floor. Margaret shoots a look at Joy, as if she was the one that did it.

She's not much of a dog person, Erica says.

No shit? Joy laughs.

Come here, come here boy! Erica sits in the grass and Bernie runs over, giddy to have been invited for play.

Erica, Frankie shouts over, the grass is all gross and wet.

Erica shrugs her shoulders and wrestles the ball out of Bernie's mouth, throws it down the garden for him. She holds her hand out to Joy who pulls her back up.

Your dog is amazing, she says, I wish I could get one in my place - our place, she corrects herself.

He's my best mate, how sad is that?

Not sad at all.

They both sip their wines and watch as Bernie tosses the ball up in the air for himself.

A burst of laughter from the group behind them interrupts her wandering thought path. She and Erica exchange glances.

Looks like this lot aren't gonna have any issues getting along today, who'd have thought?

I think Margaret is so fascinated by hair extensions that she's forgotten that Frankie likes pussy.

Erica spits her wine onto the grass, looks at Joy with wide eyed disbelief, before letting out a snort of laughter.

The pair stand together trying to contain their cackles, like misbehaving school kids. Seb catches Joy's eye, an inquisitive look on his face. She slows down her laughter and checks her watch.

I need to get back to the kitchen, she says matter of fact.

Erica notices her shift in mood, sees Seb looking over at them.

I'll help you out, she says. I don't much fancy a conversation about hair extensions anyways.

Joy nods and calls for Bernie, the three of them retreat to the house together. Joy can still feel Seb's eyes burning into her back.

As soon as they are through the doors to the garden, Erica asks the question.

Does he know? About us, I mean?

Joy checks on the oven and busies herself preparing the kitchen aid, ready to mix the potatoes with butter and salt.

Joy? Did you not tell him?

Joy takes a gulp of her wine and slumps into a chair at the island.

Half and half, she says.

What in the fuck does that mean? How do you half tell your husband about having an *ex-girlfriend*?

No, no. He knows I've had a girlfriend. He just…

He doesn't know it was me.

Joy shuffles uncomfortably in her seat.

Yeah.

Wow.

Look, it just wasn't necessary information when I met him. He didn't know you; I didn't think I'd ever even hear from you again, let alone have you in my mother-in-law's house for a fucking roast dinner. It didn't seem important.

Erica flinches.

Not that *you* weren't important. Aren't important. You are, it just- it never came up. I can't explain it properly. But he doesn't know it was you, and he can get kind of jealous, it's probably just best if he doesn't know still.

Erica nods.

Sure, okay.

Please, don't be upset with me.

I'm not, I'm not. It's just weird. Like you've erased that part of our history.

That's not true, E. It's still very real to me.

Me too, she replies, softening at the use of her old nickname.

Joy reaches over and puts her hand on top of Erica's, strokes it with her thumb.

Look, Er-

Oooooh, am I interrupting something? Valencia appears in the doorway, has taken off her heels already. Joy pulls her hand away.

Ignore me, I'm not here, I just need more vino. Val points towards the fridge and covers her eyes with her hand theatrically.

There's nothing to see, you tit.

Erica throws a tea towel at her.

Val laughs and pulls two bottles of wine from the fridge, winks at Joy and Erica.

Good to see you two getting on again. She waves a manicured hand in their direction and floats back out of the doors, announcing the arrival of more alcohol to the cheers of the group outside.

So, Erica says, mash?

Mash. You drain the potatoes; I'll grab the butter. The stuffing can probably come out soon, too.

They work in harmony preparing the last of the food and adding the finishing touches to the dining table, Erica sneaking tastes of everything as they go.

You got better at cooking, you know. Remember when you'd make us cheese toasties when we were hungover? With beans inside?

Don't start talking shit about cheesy bean toasties, I won't hear of it. Joy jabs Erica with a wooden spoon.

Just saying, you've gone up in the world.

Well, I'm still me.

They smile at each other, Joy feeling more like herself than she has in a long time.

The timer shrilly informs them that the last of the food is ready. They both cover their hands with tea towels and transport everything into the dining room, laying it out in the middle of the table.

Good work, Erica says.

Team effort, Joy replies as they clink their glasses together once more, tipsy now.

Joy piles Bernie's food into his bowl and settles him on his bed in the hallway. She calls out of the kitchen doors that dinner is ready, feeling like some strange grunge version of Florence Henderson.

As they all settle around the dining table, the atmosphere is light and happy. Just what she wanted. She looks over at Erica, who has been pulled into conversation with Margaret and Frankie. She makes eye contact with her, a subtle eye roll. Joy smiles and loads her plate up with food. Cauliflower cheese and roasted potatoes, honey and garlic carrots, sage and onion stuffing.

Well, it's no cheesy bean toastie, Erica says as she swallows a mouthful, but fuck me it's good.

Joy snorts a laugh and claps her hand over her mouth. Erica always got loose lipped after a few drinks, Joy always found it hilarious. She surveys the expressions at the table, Seb with his disapproving gaze, eyes boring into Joy as if she is the one who swore in front of his delicate Mother. Val's mouth slightly ajar in amusement, waiting for a reaction. Margaret stares daggers at Erica, and then Joy. Erica happily and obliviously pours gravy into a Yorkshire pudding.

So, Joy, Margaret says pointedly. Tell me, how do you and Emma know each other?

Val chokes slightly on a carrot, Seb slaps her on the back.

Not Emma, Erica, Joy corrects her.

Erica, apologies.

The question sounds innocent, but Joy detects an undertone. She shoots a glance over at Val, who communicates *I don't know how to help you* through her eyes.

We met in art college, Joy replies.

I see, how wonderful that you have stayed friends all these years.

Yes, Joy says flatly, carries on eating her dinner.

Back in my day, she continues, a woman who fancied men wouldn't be caught dead being chummy with a lesbian, people would talk.

Well, Joy says, thankfully things have changed. She pushes her fingernails into the palm of her hand underneath the table.

Seb clears his throat.

We should nip down to the pub later, no? What does everyone think?

After a small silence, everybody mumbles their agreement. Situation de-escalated, Seb turns back to his food. Joy is grateful for him in that moment, united in their unwillingness to explain Joy's bisexuality to his mother.

The table returns to its small conversations, Joy makes the mistake of catching Margaret's eye. She can't quite place the expression, but feels like an ant under a magnifying glass. She watches her mother-in-law drain her prosecco glass and top it back up, before she turns to Erica.

So, she says as Joy braces herself, when are you going to be popping the question to this lovely lady, Erica?

Margaret leans into Frankie and clinks glasses with her, a coy smile on her lips.

Oh, Erica stumbles, we haven't really, well, we-

I haven't long moved in, Frankie cuts in.

Yeah, it's not been so long yet.

Yeah. So probably within the next year I'd say, Frankie says with a smile.

That long? Margaret asks. In my day, you'd expect a proposal before moving in with a chap, make sure they're serious.

Frankie smiles politely and carries on poking at her dinner, unaware of the look of horror on Erica's face.

You've done well with this one, Margaret says to Erica, she will look fabulous with a big rock on that finger.

Margaret sips from her drink, smile still fixed there, as if she knows the chaos she is inciting within Erica's head, as if she can't see Erica white knuckling her cutlery.

Well, Seb announces, his voice booming and deep. I think that meal deserves a congratulations to my talented wife.

He raises his wine glass.

To Joy.

To Joy, everyone repeats.

Seb kisses Joy on the head, an act of intimacy that takes her by surprise. She blushes, hating the spotlight, tries to make eye contact with Erica but her gaze is fixed firmly on her empty plate. She feels as though she wants to apologise to her for having to witness such an intimate moment.

She does not understand her own reasoning for this. Erica is here with her girlfriend. Her sweet, beautiful, charming girlfriend at that, who seems to be expecting a proposal. And yet, she feels disloyal to her somehow. As if showing affection towards her own husband is somehow betraying the moments that they have shared today. Val drains her glass.

Erica and Frankie get out of their seats to help Joy clear the table, Margaret grabs onto Frankie's hand and waves with the other.

Don't bother yourself with that, dear.

I should probably help, Frankie says.

No, no. You sit here with me. She pats the seat that Frankie just got out of.

Tell me more about those nails of yours, how do you manage with them being so long?

Joy quiets the rage inside of her at being treated like a housekeeper, shoves it down.

She gets out of her chair with a forced smile, collects the empty wine bottles off of the

table. She mumbles that she is going to get some more from the kitchen, leaves the room before anybody can respond. She pulls a fresh bottle out of the fridge and pours herself a large glass, takes three big gulps.

Erica appears in the doorway holding the dirty plates.

Thank you, Joy says.

Erica dumps the pile on the kitchen island, licks a bit of gravy off her finger that has spilled over from one of them.

She's a bit rotten, isn't she. Erica points her thumb in the direction of the dining room.

Joy nods, picks a leftover roast potato out of the tray and pops it into her mouth. The unexpected heat causes her to spit it back out immediately, it drops to the floor.

Sexy, Erica says.

Their laughter is interrupted as Frankie walks into the kitchen.

She walks up and joins in their laughter, which ebbs out. She puts an arm around Erica.

What's going on in here then?

Ah, nothing, just being daft, Erica says.

I'm just getting Margaret a sherry, she's really nice, isn't she?

Joy scoffs. Yeah, a treasure.

Frankie tilts her head in confusion.

Do you not like her? she asks. She's been really sweet to me. Although I wouldn't mind getting a chance to talk to Val. But she's been really cute.

Cute? Erica asks.

Frankie shrugs her shoulders in the sweet way that she does, her pearly smile wide on her face.

Don't judge a book by its cover, babe, you know that.

I mean, the book seems a bit homophobic, but sure.

Frankie narrows her eyes at Erica.

She was just asking about when we are going to get *married,* babe. I don't think a homophobic person would do that.

Erica opens the dishwasher and starts stacking it. Joy retreats to the sink to rinse some glasses, doesn't want to be in the middle of whatever this is. The tension in the air thickens.

You're the one that wanted to come today, so the least you could do is pretend to enjoy yourself, maybe talk to more than one person. Maybe not act like somebody has just threatened to murder your firstborn when asked about proposing to me.

I just… I wasn't expecting the question, that's all.

She flits her eyes in Joy's direction, who catches it in her peripherals, but doesn't dare to look up from the sink.

With that, Frankie exits the kitchen, a bottle of sherry in hand and a trail of cold air behind her.

A breath out, and they finish cleaning up in silence. When there is nothing left to wash up or wipe down, Joy pours them another wine each, offers Erica a cigarette.

Bernie follows them into the garden, the late afternoon air now biting, darkness settling over the city. The darkness triggers the solar sensors, creating an intricate web of tiny warm white lights that frame the garden. Joy and Erica settle on a swing seat by the chiminea, some embers still fighting to give off heat.

Got a light? Erica asks.

Joy reaches into her pocket and brings out the neon lighter, worn smiley face still visible, staring up at them.

I can't believe you still have this, Erica says. Surely it belongs in a museum of some sort by now.

Joy ignites the flame and cups it with her free hand, lights the end of Erica's cigarette and then her own.

It must be some sort of record by now, no way I'm getting rid of it.

It's nice out here, Erica says as she blows a long stream of smoke into the air, turning her attention to the manicured lawn.

Yeah, they have a gardener, surprise surprise. Although I did bully Margaret into the fairy lights last week. Gardens look dull without them, in my opinion.

Agreed. It always reminds of that Halloween party, remember?

Joy knows exactly which party Erica is referring to, but can't bring herself to do anything other than nod. Isn't sure her heart can handle a trip down memory lane.

I thought you were the coolest person I'd ever met back then; Erica continues.

Am I not now? Joy recoils in fake offense.

Shut up, you still are, obviously. It's different though, isn't it. Things are different now.

Joy nods. Things are indeed different now.

I think about it a lot, you know. About what right now might be like if I'd never run away from Brighton years ago.

Well, you ran away from me, E. Not Brighton.

Erica takes a long drag on her cigarette and stubs it out on the bottom of her shoe, looks at the floor for a while.

I'm sorry about that, for what it's worth.

Joy throws the end of her cigarette into the chiminea.

I'm sorry for not stopping you, I was such a twat back then.

They let the silence linger between them, embers crackling in the fire in front of them.

Christ, we know how to have a good time, don't we?

Erica nudges Joy with her hand, lets it rest next to hers on the seat. Their fingers touch, each moving a little more until they are entwined. A feeling of nostalgic familiarity washes over both of them, that perfect fit that always felt like home.

They sit, staring ahead, neither wanting the moment to end nor wanting to know what it means.

Are you really going to prop-

Joy?

Seb's voice echoes through the garden interrupting them, they pull their hands away immediately as Joy stands up and waves at him.

We're going to head to the pub, come on.

Okay, she says. Seb reaches out his hand as she approaches the back door, she takes it, it suddenly feels rough, uninviting, not right.

Erica follows behind, calls Bernie in with her. They cannot make eye contact with each other.

Frankie, seemingly over the disagreement they had in the kitchen, offers Erica her furry coat.

Come on, babe, it's freezing outside. She pulls it around Erica and clasps her manicured hands over hers.

Your hands are like ice, Frankie says as she blows warm air from her mouth onto them.

Joy watches as this kind and loving act unfolds in front of her, while fire surges in the depths of her stomach. Jealously? Anger? Indigestion? She doesn't want to know. Not tonight. As they all get ready to leave the house, Joy pulls out six shot glasses, fills them with an old tequila she found in Margaret's drinks cabinet a few days prior.

Hold up, she says. One for the road.

Everyone takes a glass, including Margaret.

What are we toasting to? Asks Val.

To love, Erica says, catching Joy's gaze.

They repeat the sentiment and down the shots, leave the house in a collection of furry coats, woolly scarves and designer hats.

Joy watches as Erica organises earmuffs around her hair bun, her intoxicating laugh like music to her ears.

To love, she thinks.

To love.

21

2016 / BRIGHTON

Val had spent hours poring over different outfits, unsure which one would convey the correct sense of educated but also very sexy at the same time. She had eventually settled on a little red number, bunched at her tiny waist, accentuating her bony hips. When they had handed her the robe, she had initially refused to wear it, but relented when Joy and Meg put theirs on.

You still look better than everyone else here, the girls had told her.

Joy had opted for a black dress, predictably. Seb had taken her shopping for the perfect graduation dress, insisting that she have something new and memorable on her special day. She had eventually relented and let him buy her the outfit. A simple and sleek LBD. She had learnt that abbreviation from the sales assistant who couldn't keep her eyes off of Seb.

With Meg in a bright pink pantsuit, the three of them stood for a picture together. An eclectic rainbow of different styles, different people, different plans for the future.

Val had a train booked straight back to Liverpool for the next morning. Her Dad had an apartment on the Albert Dock all set up and ready for her. Her degree now a picture on the wall, she was focussed entirely on her new 'influencer' title. Sponsorships from fashion brands, makeup brands, even restaurants, all throwing money in her direction if she would advertise their products. The 'vegan health' reputation she had spent so long building up was gaining traction in mainstream media, young women all looking up to people just like her. Joy and Megan were forbidden from ever mentioning her love of pepperoni.

Meg was intent on staying in Brighton with her Mum. She had been offered a job at one of her friends' pottery studios, which suited her down to the ground. She could move back into her Mum's house for free, work short hours, and be within spitting distance of her favourite bars and clubs, not yet ready to grow up.

Joy was torn. Her Dad, having made his excuses for not coming across the country for her graduation, was still in Liverpool. She couldn't go back. She pushed the thought of Erica away, once again. Nothing was waiting for her there.

Seb beamed proudly behind the camera. Their relationship now two years old, he was living and working in London, coming to see her on weekends. She knew in the back of her mind that she'd move to be with him. What other choice was there?

*

The post-graduation party was at the girls' flat. One last hurrah in the place they had called home for the last couple of years. They had strewn it with confetti and balloons, spent the last of their final grant money on a case of prosecco. Joy had spent the night before cooking a giant pot of vegetable chilli. She set out paper plates next to the pot, along with plastic cups and cutlery. None of them intended on cleaning the mess after the party, so they ensured it could all be thrown away.

Come ten o'clock, the flat was full of their nearest and dearest, all merry and dancing.

I'm so proud of you, Seb shouted into Joy's ear above the music.

She beamed back at him, noticed him fumbling with something in his pocket. He looked nervous. She shot a look over to Val, but she was wrapped up in an intense looking conversation with one of their professors who had somehow made his way to the party. Was that allowed?

Joy, there's something I've been meaning to ask you, Seb started.

Panic shot from Joy's stomach to the roof of her mouth, her hands suddenly clammy. She dropped her plastic cup of wine, spilling its contents onto her dress.

Shit! Sorry, Seb, let me go clean this up, back in a mo.

She pulled an apologetic face and backed away to the bathroom, Seb none the wiser as he stood awkwardly with one hand on the item in his pocket, the inevitable on the tip of his tongue.

Joy pushed past people to get to the bathroom, barricaded herself inside.

She leant against the door and took deep breaths, tried to calm herself. She had suspected this was coming sometime soon, what with him being older than her and them possibly moving in together. But, fuck. She felt blindsided.

She slid to the floor and closed her eyes, let her breath become normal again, tried to ignore the rising nausea. Did she want this? This didn't seem like a natural reaction to a man wanting to marry you. She told herself it was nerves, but something buried deep inside of her knew what it really was.

She pulled out her phone, straight to Facebook. She pulled up Erica's profile, ran her thumb across her profile picture. Her heart dropped to her stomach as she saw the update. Single.

She stared at the word for a moment. Single. Erica was single. Something had happened with the perfect reindeer girl and now she was gone. Joy let her thoughts process, tried to work out what to do as quickly as possible. She took another deep breath.

Resolute, she stood up, didn't bother wiping the spillage from herself. She had to get out of here, had to pack a bag, get on a train and go and see Erica. Never in her life had she been so sure of something.

She unlocked the bathroom door, ready to battle her way back to Seb, to ruin his night, to ruin everything they'd built. Where was everyone? It was as if an evacuation had taken place in the five minutes she'd sat in the bathroom.

She peered into the kitchen, nothing. The bedrooms were empty too.

A feeling of dread slowly rose from within her as she turned the corner into the living room. All of her friends, everyone at the party, stood looking at her expectantly, smiles on their faces. At the front of them, Seb, on one knee.

My darling Joy, he said as he reached for her to come closer.

Will you do me the absolute honour, in front of friends, of agreeing to be my wife?

The atmosphere stilled as he awaited her response, the air thick with his anticipation, his smug smile that indicated he already expected her to say yes.

She looked up at their friends, some dramatically wiping tears from their eyes. Val looked shocked; her mouth slightly ajar.

Well, Seb, thank you. It's just… well… the thing is–

He looked into her eyes, unaware of the internal conflict within her.

Yes? He whispered.

I… I…

She couldn't embarrass him in this way, couldn't believe he'd done this to her, that she was about to do this to herself.

S–sure, she stuttered.

She said YES! He cheered, as the music blasted back on and the room went crazy.

Seb slipped the diamond on her finger, the weight of it a reminder of everything she just lost. Everything she would never have.

22

2019 / LIVERPOOL

<3 HALLOWEEN 2019 <3
31/10/19
YOU ARE INVITED!
@ THE PEN FACTORY, HOPE STREET
DRESS UP OR DON'T SHOW UP
CATERED, LET ME KNOW UR DIETARY DEETS
RSVP ASAP!
<3 V <3

Val shoots the message off to everyone on her list before throwing herself back onto her sofa. The empty wrappers underneath her dig into her back. She burps into her hand; it tastes like pickled onion monster munch and Kit Kats. Since she called it quits with Seb, she hasn't been able to function, not properly. Eating has been her comfort, as it always has been, something she can control. She thumbs the plaster that she has stuck over her most recent thigh incision.

The Sunday at Margaret's had been just about bearable, even with Seb doing the devoted husband act. That felt cruel, Val thinks, pointed at her, an attempt to make her regret cooling things down with him. She thinks back, but can't remember a time that he has been affectionate with Joy in front of her, not since they started sleeping together regularly, at least.

Her phone buzzes in her hand, another message from him.

She has been doing an admirable job of ghosting him outside of events organised by Joy, if admirable could be a word used to describe her at all, as though her blanking him now makes up for all the years of fucking him.

She opens the text to feel the pain shoot through her insides, lets it seep into the cracks, like salt in an open wound.

Please, V, nothing weird, let's just get a drink tonight.
I miss you.

She feels the tears come, doesn't stop them. Let's them develop into quiet, deep sobs, knows that she is pulling her ugly crying face. She scrolls back on their thread, a week of him trying to contact her.

Another message comes through.

Won't even try and feel you up under the table or anything, promise.

She lets out a pathetic burst of laughter at that, her hot, salty tears making a beeline for her mouth. She looks around at the mess she has made today, thinks it is reminiscent of the chaos inside her mind, then berates herself for being so self-indulgent.

Her fingers hover over the screen. She already knows what she is going to do, but allowing herself a few seconds of pretending otherwise lets her think herself torn, tortured.

Carpathia, 7pm.

Immediately he sends back a smiley face and thumbs up emoji. She can picture his face now, smug happiness, relief, perhaps a slight panic as he decides which lie, he is going to spin to his wife tonight. She will believe it, she always does. At least she pretends to.

In the years that Val has known Joy, she has never understood her blind spot with Seb. They didn't make sense as a couple in uni, but it was passed off as a fling. It didn't make sense when they got engaged, when Joy uprooted her potential in Brighton and moved to London, when he started making excuses for entire weekends with Val, how she would just accept the information and turn a blind eye. Val often wonders if Joy is aware, and just doesn't care enough to say anything, knows that that is wishful thinking, that she only hopes for that scenario so that she will never have to find out properly what her oldest friend has been doing behind her back.

She lets her phone drop to the floor and mentally goes through all the outfits that she could wear this evening. Something incredible, she thinks, something that will make him eat his heart out. She stands up, dusts the wrappers off of herself, wraps her hair into a bun to keep it dry in the shower. Her stomach groans with the weight of what she has eaten; she sighs, the inevitable about to happen. She leaves her phone on the ground, lighting up with peoples excited replies to her invite, and closes the bathroom door behind her.

23

2017 / SOMEWHERE IN THE COTSWOLDS

Joy leant against the brick wall of the manor house and let the cool evening breeze hit her face. She felt sticky from dancing, flushed from the wine, hoped that she hadn't gotten any of it on her dress, the night now able to conceal any stains on the white lace.

Val appeared in front of her, a vision in gold and silk, and lit the cigarette hanging from Joy's lips. She exhaled the smoke into the air.

Well, Val said as she leant next to her, you did it.

I did it.

That's like, the least dramatic wedding I've ever attended. Not one family fight, no catering nightmares, no drunken speeches, no topless bridesmaids… yet, anyway.

Sorry to disappoint, Joy laughed.

Shut up, it's been a great day.

Joy nodded, closed her eyes, and took a deep drag of her cigarette.

Did you manage to eat today? Everyone always says the bride never gets the chance to eat.

Yeah, a little. Think Margaret would have actually murdered me if I'd not sampled the billion quid catering that she's holding over me. People loved it, I think.

Mm.

You going to tell me what's up, babes?

Joy looked at her then with tired eyes, and Val's heart hurt for her.

It's just… over now, isn't it?

What is?

Everything. Everything outside of Seb, it's over. Uni is over, our flat is over, you're back in Liverpool, I'm getting the Stepford Wife treatment in London, I'm just somebody's wife now. I don't even have a job, V.

Well, you could get one if you wanted?

But I don't need to, do I? I've married smart, as I've heard at least six of the old wrinkled handbags in that room say today.

And… you're upset about that?

No, not upset, I don't know. It's not like I didn't know that before today. It's probably just the stress of the day or something. I just…

Joy slid down the wall and sat on the gravel below, no longer caring about the state of her dress, stubbed her cigarette out between the rocks. With some careful rearranging of her outfit, Val did the same.

Is it Erica?

Joy squeezed her eyes closed, took a deep breath.

It can't be.

Well, if it is, you could just talk to her and–

I literally just, today, got married, V. It doesn't matter anymore.

They were both silent for a moment, listening to the sound of inebriated guests shouting goodbyes to each other, the music echoing from the reception somewhere behind them.

Seb loves you.

I know.

You're going to be happy in London, I just know it.

You're going to visit, right?

Of course.

Joy took Val's hand then, squeezed it tight.

You know, Val said, over the years that we've known each other, I've seen you spend the majority of them pine for this girl that you were with for less than a year. That always seemed crazy to me, that somebody could have that effect on you in such a short space of time. I met her, I saw you guys together, and I did get it, I understood. But it never happened, not really, it just wasn't meant to be.

Joy stared at the ground in front of them.

And I don't say this to be mean, you know I love you, but I have to agree with the wrinkled handbags. You've married well.

Joy nodded then.

Thank you.

Anytime. Wanna go drink the leftover fizz and find somebody for me to take home?

Absolutely.

Val got to her feet, took Joy's hand and pulled her up, helped her swipe the gravel bits off her dress, and hugged her tight.

You're a great friend, V.

I know, I'm brilliant. Let's get you back in there before they all think you've jilted the poor lad.

Joy and Val linked arms and walked back into the reception together, greeted by the sounds of leftover drunken guests. Joy spotted Seb dancing with his inebriated Mum, twirling her around by her hand to a remixed version of Elvis' 'Can't help falling in love with you'. He looked up, a slight pang of shock on his face at seeing Joy and Val together, as if he'd somehow forgotten that they were both in attendance. He waved them over, cheeks red from dancing and too much top shelf indulgence. He took Joy's hand as they got close.

Val took Margaret's hand and led her towards the bar to get another martini. Seb pulled Joy close, a hand on the small of her back.

So, wife, he said into her ear.

Yes, husband? She replied.

Good day?

Eh, so-so, she shrugged as he took her hand above her head and spun her around, a wicked grin on her face as he manoeuvred her body back into his.

Oh, I see, just average, yes? He asked, hips against hers as they moved to the music together.

How about you? Good day?

The best.

He spun her to face him then, kissed her gently. She smiled up at him then let her head rest on his chest, as they swayed to the final bars of Elvis's baritone.

24

2019 / LIVERPOOL

FACEBOOK MESSENGER

JOY: got Val's invite?
ERICA: Yep, dreading it already.
JOY: yeah right, you loooove a reason to dress up.
ERICA: any ideas what you're going as?
JOY: no spoilers here, sorry.
ERICA: intriguing...
ERICA: you okay?
JOY: feel a bit shit, headache and stuff.
ERICA: hangover?
JOY: I wish, not done anything fun all week.
ERICA: same.
JOY: plans tonight?
ERICA: nah, Frankie is out with her friends, I'm about to watch homes under the hammer.
JOY: you're wild.
ERICA: I was always the cool one.
JOY: sureeeee.
ERICA: what about you? Plans?
JOY: nah, Seb's out with his old mates again, Margaret is at some bingo night. One of her undead pals came and picked her up earlier, wheeled her away.
ERICA: your broken mother-in-law is having more fun than you?

Tragic
JOY: right?! Eurgh. I started making lasagne earlier, gonna pop it in the oven. Least if I'm miserable I have a giant slab of that to keep me company.
ERICA: Sounds amazing, I'm jealous. Microwave meal for me ☺
JOY: I'll save you some, admission is two bottles of wine hahah.
ERICA: calling uber now.
JOY: hahaha
JOY: ...wait, really?

*

The doorbell rings twenty minutes later. Joy opens it in disbelief, and although she did brush her hair and throw on some makeup on the off chance that Erica was serious, she cannot believe her eyes when she is stood in the doorway, a bottle of wine in each hand, a dimpled smile on her face.

The sight fills Joy with emotion, she wants to cry and hug her and kiss her and shut the door in her face all in one moment. Instead, she just opens the door wider, allowing her to step inside. Bernie greets Erica first, bounding out of the kitchen at the sight of a guest. She hands Joy the wine and gets down on the floor, lets him bounce around her, gleefully accepting the attention that Erica offers him. The sight of them together fills her heart up to bursting, just as it did when they were all in the house last Sunday.

Erica gets up and surveys Joy's appearance.

You look great, sick my arse.

Sod off, I look like a corpse.

You always look like a corpse, that's like, your thing, no?

Joy shoves her in the side of the ribs and leads them all into the kitchen. The irresistible smell of freshly baked lasagne hits Erica immediately, her stomach growls in response.

That smells fucking insane, she says as she peers through the oven door.

Right? Kind of gutted that I have to share it.

Erica makes a face of faux offense.

Girl, I can call an uber and be right back at my place in the click of a button.

Ha, I'm kidding, I'm glad you're here.

Me too.

They fill up a wine glass each and clink them together.

Thank God you bought this, I was so close to drinking Sebs red.

Ewwww, grown up Ribena? No thanks.

Exactly. Gross.

Joy gestures for Erica to sit at the kitchen island, laden with candles, cutlery and Margaret's overpriced placemats. She pulls garlic bread out of the oven, cuts it into thick slices and places it all onto a board. She slips the oven gloves onto her hands and pulls the bubbling lasagne out of the oven, places it between them.

Right, she says with a spatula in her hand, let's get stuck into this.

*

An hour later and the lasagne is gone, along with the two bottles of wine. Joy and Erica sit back in their chairs, full to bursting. Souixsie Sioux sings out from the speakers, an alternative eighties playlist that Joy has spent years curating.

Okay, I'm sorry, but this is happening, Erica says as she undoes the button and zipper on her skinny jeans to release her full stomach. She lets out a satisfied groan.

It's official, you make the best food. I have no idea how Seb isn't the size of a house.

Ha, yeah right. He's far too vain for that.

Mm, Frankie is the same, never lets herself enjoy food, it's just for pictures mostly.

Alien to me, that is.

Same. Ciggie?

Ooooh, yeah.

Joy gets up and fetches two thick weave blankets from the living room, along with a bottle of Seb's red wine. She shouts Bernie and taps her leg; he jumps out of his bed and follows her through the patio doors into the crisp night.

Looks like we're stuck with it, Joy says as she shows Erica the bottle of Rioja.

Eurgh, fine. Better than nothing I suppose.

They both take a seat on the outdoor sofa and wrap the blankets around themselves. Bernie lies at their feet, too tired for more play.

So, Joy says. You're proposing to Frankie, apparently?

Ha, yeah, it seems that way. Erica busies herself pouring them glasses of wine, takes the cork in her hand and picks at it with her nails.

You seem super happy about it, Joy says.

Well, it's not really been my decision, Frankie just kind of expects it to happen.

You should just tell her how you feel, be honest.

Ha, not sure you're one to be doling out honest relationship advice.

Joy sits up straight.

What's that supposed to mean?

No, nothing, not like that. It's just, well, you're not exactly *happy*, are you?

How the hell would you know if I'm happy or not? I've been back here for about five minutes.

Erica sips her wine, winces, hates the taste of red.

Sorry, it's just, with Frankie, I thought I knew what I wanted. But then the last few weeks with you-

Please don't.

Joy, come on, I think we need talk about how we're feeling.

I don't know what you're feeling, but don't project it onto me.

Erica puts her wine down on the table in front of them, turns to look at Joy.

So, I've just made it all up in my head then, have I? The little looks, the spark every time we accidentally touch each other? Are you seriously going to sit there and tell me that I'm the only one who can feel this?

Joy sits silently for a while, before speaking in a small voice.

I'm married, E.

So?! What does that even mean? Where even is your husband right now? From what I can see, you have no idea, and rarely do. He just left you here to go out fuck knows where. Who is here for you? Me, I am. Just like I always have been.

That's bullshit.

Oh, yeah? Enlighten me.

You haven't always been here for me, E. Not sure if you recall, but you fucked off as quickly as you could the second, I got new friends back when we were together. I was so lonely after you left, and you wouldn't even answer my calls? My messages, ignored, you didn't even bother to check if I was okay after you just fucking vanished that night.

I didn't fucking vanish, Joy, I was hurt, upset. Don't try and tell me about lonely, you have no idea. You had spent that whole day acting like some stuck up bitch that I didn't recognise, and all I wanted to do was spend time with you, that's all I ever wanted to do. It's all I want to do now.

Well, you've a funny way of showing it.

Do I? Because I think I'm the one that just pitched up here at a second's notice, the one that jumped at the opportunity to spend the evening with you and carry on this weird pretend-a-thon that we are both participating in.

I've just been hanging out with you as friends, it doesn't mean anything else.

Joy stares into her wine, fights hard to keep tears at bay.

Erica looks at her.

Do you really mean that, Joy? I don't mean anything else to you?

I'm married. You are with Frankie. There's no point in-

Bullshit! That's absolute bullshit, and you know it. Yeah,

you're married, so, what? You're just going to stay with him forever, regardless of how unhappy you are? Regardless of how you feel about me? Of how we feel about each-other?

Joy takes a steady breath in, wipes her eyes.

I can't do this, Erica. You need to leave.

Without another word, Erica stands up and throws down her blanket. Bernie rises with her, but she ignores him. Just looks at Joy, waiting for her to look back.

She does not.

It's the second time you've hurt me, Joy. I won't let you do it again.

Joy lets tears fall onto her hands as she hears the patio door slam, the front door open and close. She drains her glass and pulls Bernie onto the seat with her, sobs into his soft fur.

She let Erica leave, just like she did in Brighton.

She pushes down the immediate regret and pulls herself together. Gathers the blankets, the undrunk wine, turns off the fairy lights. She pulls out a cigarette and lights it up, the battered neon smiley face on the lighter staring up at her, judging her.

Her phone comes to life in her hand, a call from Seb.

She inhales deeply before answering, he can't know she's upset.

Hey, you okay?

No response, just the busy background blur of a crowded bar. Has he pocket dialled her? How is that even possible with an iPhone? She holds the phone to her ear for a minute, trying to decipher where he might be or who he could be with.

Just noise, background music of some inevitably swanky bar, some blurred laughter in the background. She hangs up.

Joy drags heavily on her cigarette and stubs it out on the decking, will deal with Margaret's wrath tomorrow. She pads back into the house and locks up, curls up on the sofa and pulls one of the blankets over herself. She wonders if Erica got home okay, if she is safe. Wants to text her, call her, tell her she was right and kiss her until their mouths are sore.

She falls asleep alone.

25

OCTOBER 14TH 2019 / LIVERPOOL

GROUP CHAT: SPOOKY GALS ☺<3

VAL: So! What're you guys wearing for the party?
VAL: hello?
VAL: helllooooooooooo?
ERICA: Sorry V, not sure yet. Franks is thinking of a couple's costume, cue vomit emoji.
VAL: happy wife, happy life.
ERICA: haha very funny.
VAL: I think I'm going to do a Halloween classic, just a cat, you know? Sexy, unoffensive.
ERICA: Sounds good.
VAL: joy what about u???
VAL: JOOOOOOY?
JOY: Hey, actually Seb's mom is doing pretty good, she said we can go home next week if we want to. She's got this full-time care person, says we're never around anyway. So, we might not even be here for it :/
VAL: unacceptable! I'm texting Seb right now, you're not allowed to miss it!
VAL: Right erica?!
VAL: I got this amazing caterer for the food, it's gonna be all veggie and vegan stuff, come oooooon you guys, you can't bail!
JOY: Seb just got your text, he said we can wait until after

the party before going back to London.

VAL: YAAAAAAY!!!! Now, go find some costumes. Love you both xxxx

JOY: Love you.

26

OCTOBER 20TH 2019 / LIVERPOOL

Joy holds in a frustrated scream as the second child in the past five minutes runs past her, stomping on her feet in the process. She smiles tightly as the mother follows, mouthing her apologies. Seb looks on from beside her.

And you want one of those? Mental.

He scoffs, shoves her gently.

They have had the conversation many times, Joy has made sure he's known from day one that she doesn't want children. He has always claimed to want the same thing as her, but she can see the look in his eye.

So, you need one of these? She asks, as she hands him a box containing an oversized hypodermic needle.

Yep, perfect. I can just use the scrubs I have at Mum's.

And that's definitely what you want to be? Literally just like… your own job?

Problem?

No, no problem.

Sorry if that's not *cool* enough for you.

He stalks off to the counter to pay, leaving her feeling like a bitch.

She checks her phone for what feels like the billionth time this week. Nothing from Erica, besides their group chat with Val. Instagram and Facebook updates from Frankie have shown them out at restaurants together all week, cocktail bars and the cinema. Joy suspects that she is trying to orchestrate her own proposal moment. A sinking sick feeling descends upon Joy at the thought of Erica asking Frankie to marry her.

She wonders if this is how Erica felt when she found out that Joy was marrying Seb. Remembers what she was going to do the night that Seb proposed, how ready she was to leave it all behind and go to Erica.

She shakes it off, goes to the counter to pay.

Joy finds Seb waiting outside for her, the queue mounting beside him. Smiffy's Costume Shop has always been chaos during October, as far back as she can remember. She has always loved how seriously people take Halloween here.

Got everything?

Yep.

Shall we get some lunch or something?

Can't, got to nip into the surgery.

Ah, okay. I'll just head home then, shall I?

Sure. You sure you're okay? You look a bit… peaky.

Bit flustered, that's all. Too busy in there.

Right, well if you're coming down with something then stay away from Mum.

Shall do.

They kiss briefly and part ways, Joy holding both of their bags in her hands. She pushes her way through the crowds of Bold Street towards the Liverpool One car park, which seems like miles away.

A wave of panic and nausea hits her, she sits on a bench near the bustling Primark. She takes some deep breaths in and out, calms herself, digs her nails into the palm of her hand.

You alright there, girl?

A nearby man shouts over from his spot on the ground, sheltered from the cold by several coats, a small dog wrapped in a blanket on his lap.

Yep, yeh, all good thank you, she shouts back.

He nods suspiciously and then returns his attention to passers-by. She sits back and takes in her surroundings, a busy day in the city centre. She continues her deep breaths, well-practiced over the years, as she observes the crowd outside of Primark. Impatient men waiting for their wives, daughters, friends, refusing to go past the threshold. Seagulls getting dangerously close to tourists who are either brave enough or stupid enough to eat their Greggs whilst walking. Joy used to love watching the ferocious birds steal pasties right out of the hands of unsuspecting people. She smiles as a pair of teenagers attempt to bat the seagulls away, before launching half a McDonalds cheeseburger onto the floor, allowing them a safe escape.

The usual sounds of the busy city centre carry on around her. Children crying from their prams or at their parents' sides, bored and tired of shopping, wanting to go home. The people spilling out of the Wetherspoons for cigarettes, wobbly on their feet, already jostling for a fight. No doubt they would later migrate to Matthew Street for karaoke and a punch up, or to Concert Square to try it on with the young students.

This bit of the city used to make her anxious. Unless there is a need to shop, it is usually avoided by locals due to its busy nature, the presence of obnoxious tourists, drunks and students. Today she breathes it in. Her city, the one she so readily abandoned, is thriving. It's heart beating so loud that it echoes, draws people back to it over and over again.

She stands up and hands the concerned man on the ground some change from her pocket, he thanks her in his thick Liverpudlian accent. She swallows the nausea and panic and carries on towards the car park, dodging prams, skateboarding teenagers and slow walkers until she gets to her car. Her heart leaps into her throat every time she spots someone in the distance with orange hair, so she walks with her eyes down instead. Her phone vibrates in her hand.

GROUP CHAT: SPOOKY GALS☺<3

VAL: Here's my costume! What do you think??? X

Val sends through a picture of her wearing a shiny black body suit, strapless, complete with a huge pair of fluffy cat ears. Joy smiles at the image, her beautiful friend.

JOY: Meoowwwww, you look amazing in that!
VAL: Thanks, hoping that dressing as a cat isn't like, offensive in any way??? There's always that one person in the insta comments that just wants to make me look stupid.
JOY: think you're safe with that one.
ERICA: looking great, v.
VAL: have you decided what you are yet?
VAL: let me rephrase that; Erica, has Frankie told you what you're coming as yet?
ERICA: would be funny if it wasn't true, yes, she has.
VAL: do tell???
ERICA: sworn to secrecy.
VAL: omg I'm so excited!
JOY: yeah, me too, can't be as bad as that one when we were in college lol.
ERICA IS OFFLINE

27

OCTOBER 21ST 2019 / LIVERPOOL

Valencia drags a box of decorations through the front door of the Pen Factory, one of her favourite haunts in the city. Tucked away in a cute basement, it's the perfect setting for her Halloween party. Her phone buzzes with a text from Seb. Since he and Joy have had the green light to return to London, he's wanted to see her almost every day. She can't say no. Stolen hours whilst Joy thinks he's at work, hotel rooms paid for, used for a few hours, and then abandoned, as they both go back to their own homes.

She has left party planning to the last minute, can't put it off any longer.

The niggling thought that once he's gone, he will leave her here alone, expecting her to be around waiting whenever he can sneak off for a weekend again, lingers heavy on her mind. Never a question as to whether she might be seeing somebody else, somebody single, somebody who can love her properly. A dirty night in an expensive hotel, lies on top of lies, no end game in sight. Sometimes, when they would leave those hotels after a few hours of time together and he returned to his wife, she felt nothing but cheap. Used. Val pushes the tug of loneliness inside of her away, can't think about it right now.

Fake spiderwebs and purple fairy lights peek out from the lid of the box she is carrying, and she wipes her brow with the back of her arm as a tall man with a jawline sharp enough to cut cake comes over from behind the bar to help. She thanks him and descends the small staircase into the main room.

Just tell us where you want things to be, he says in a deep voice, and we'll make sure it looks great.

Perfect, thank you, she says, trying to subtly take him in.

She pulls herself together.

The caterer should be here on the morning of, and I have someone dropping off a delivery of around eighty little ghost pumpkins too, if you could just dot them around?

Sure, he laughs.

Oh god, she bites her manicured nail. Is that weird?

Eighty tiny pumpkins? Not at all, I admire the commitment.

She blushes and pushes her hair off her face, wishes she had put more effort into her appearance before coming here.

Jack, he says as he holds out a hand for her to shake.

Valencia.

He smiles and repeats her name, dimples in his cheeks. Val feels a little flutter inside of her stomach as the syllables of her name fall off his tongue.

Ah, it's you, he says. Some of the girls here follow you on Instagram, they're excited that your party is here.

Oh, that's nice, Val says.

Super comfortable with fame, I see.

It's not fame, it's- well, I don't really know what it is.

Lost on me, my phone barely connects to the internet.

He pulls out a relic of iPhones gone by from his pocket, it still has a home button. She breathes out, he doesn't know who she is, she doesn't have to fake anything.

Fancy a drink before you head off? On the house?

Oh, Val checks her watch, I'm not sure.

She is supposed to meet Seb for an early dinner in twenty minutes, but everything inside of her is telling her to stay, to have a drink with this beautiful man.

Of course, he says, you must be so busy, another time.

She thinks of Seb, sitting, waiting for her to arrive and give him what he wants, days away from leaving her behind.

No, no, actually I'd love to.

That smile again, welcoming and warm. They take a seat at a table for two near the window. Rain is hitting the cobblestones on the patio; a group of people shelter under a big umbrella whilst they smoke.

Aren't you going to get in trouble for drinking while you're working?

Just got off, he says. What's your drink?

I'd love a glass of fizz, thank you.

Coming right up.

He leaves her with a wink, she feels herself grinning back. Her phone pings inside of her purse. Seb.

Got the table, you close?

A part of her wants to say yes. Wants to get up from the table and run to the restaurant, indulge in the familiarity of their awfulness, their betrayal. Tuck herself into that nook in his arm that she is so used to slotting into, a dirty little secret that he can't stay away from. A bigger part of her knows that she can never be happy with Seb, not really.

Fuck it, she thinks.

Sorry, can't make tonight, somethings come up! x

Val turns her phone off and slips it back inside of her bag, just as Jack reappears with two glasses of prosecco in his hands.

There we are, cheers.

They clink glasses, his eyes don't leave hers. She notices the beginnings of a tattoo on his chest, visible with a button undone.

So, this party; birthday?

Oh, no. Halloween, my favourite.

Explains the pumpkins. All eighty of them.

Well, I thought it was self-explanatory, given that it's... *on* Halloween.

Alright Sassy Pants, he says in mock offense. What're you coming as?

Guess.

He thinks for a beat.

Cat.

Val coughs as she catches some of her drink in her throat.

Yes, she says, how did you guess?

Just a… vibe I get, he replies.

She stares into the eyes of the man before her, utterly transfixed.

And you left your cat ears in the decoration box.

Val lets out a roar of laughter, people dining at the table next to them exchange glances.

Bit hasty perhaps, but I'm starving. I was about to go get some dinner; don't suppose you'd want to keep me company? Something feels dead tragic about eating alone.

She feels the weight of this decision in her stomach. Seb will have her text by now, he'll be trying to call her, getting hit with immediate voicemail, he hates it when she isn't available. He could blow the whole thing to pieces, tell Joy, post about their relationship online, ruin everything she has. She drains her glass.

I'd fucking love to.

*

Seb brings the storm inside the house with him, slamming the front door and kicking his shoes off noisily in the hallway. He finds Joy and Margaret playing chess in the living room, Bernie lying on the sofa beside them.

Darling, Margaret says. Are you okay? You look frightful.

He ignores the question and heads for the drink's cabinet, pours himself a glass of whiskey.

Do you want some food? Or did you eat with the people from work? We had jacket potatoes, there's some left in the oven. Joy points in the direction of the kitchen, as if he might not know where it is.

I ate out.

Oh, that sounds lovely, who were you with, darling? Margaret asks.

I ate by myself.

By yourself?

Yes, by myself.

You could have called me, Joy says. I'd have loved a meal out.

You're not a *prisoner*, Joy, go out if you want to. You have friends here.

Well aware of that, babe. I did message Val to see if she fancied a drink actually, but she's *met someone.*

Ooooh, Margaret says, I'm not surprised, a good-looking girl like her.

Yeah, she sent a quick text while he was in the loo, Joy laughs, met him tonight too, she seems weirdly smitten. It's cute.

Seb stares for a moment before necking his whiskey and slamming the glass down. He pours another before storming out and up to the bedroom.

Joy listens to the heavy tread of his footsteps, her husband not even trying to disguise his contempt at this news of their friend being on a date for the first time in however long. Her gut tries to speak to her, screams *you know something isn't right here, don't you?!* But instead of listening to it, she moves her Rook and lets Margaret take her Bishop. She sips her drink and tries not to think of all of the ways in which two people she loves could be betraying her. How, when she really thinks about it, she couldn't care less.

28

OCTOBER 22ND 2019 / LIVERPOOL

Val wakes up tired already, muscles aching, dry mouth from all of the cocktails. Despite this, she is happy. She rolls over and yes, she hadn't made him up, here he lies in bed next to her. Dishevelled hair, that jawline, a scar below his lip from an old piercing from his emo phase. She bites her smile, tries not to let herself get too excited.

The evening had flown by. They had walked across Hope Street and down to her one of her favourite restaurants. They shared two types of fresh pasta, eating slowly in-between endless conversations about everything. Cocktails kept on coming, and then a bottle of wine to share. They had stolen a leftover umbrella for the walk back to her apartment, him gripping her waist and holding her tightly to him to keep her safe from the rain, as if she may have melted if he'd let her get touched by it. A kiss outside of her front door, deep and knee buckling. She is suddenly aware that she is naked underneath the sheets, and that it is no longer dark. Did he see her scars? She doesn't remember him mentioning them.

Jack opens his eyes slowly, she realises too late to pretend to be sleeping, to pretend she hasn't been staring at him like some sort of stalker weirdo.

Morning, Vicky.

Val's heart sinks.

It's V-

Val, just kidding, he winks.

She pulls a pillow from beneath her and hits him with it. He grabs her with one strong arm and deposits her on top of himself. She tries to pull the sheets around her legs, but he holds her wrists and brings them to his chest. She knows he has seen.

Gorgeous, he says.

She does nothing but smile in return.

He brings her in for a kiss, she recoils.

Morning breath, no way.

She covers her mouth and runs to the bathroom; he laughs as he watches.

Don't suppose you've a spare? Can't be kissing you if you taste all minty and I taste like last night's garlic.

She rummages through her bathroom cupboard, toothbrush hanging out of her mouth, finds an unopened manual brush and throws it to him, he catches it with one hand.

So, I'm not sure, but I think we both had a good time last night?

Val spits into the sink so that she can shout her reply.

Four out of ten.

A dramatic gasp from her bed.

Okay, okay, a six.

I'll take it, he says. Any chance we can do this again? Like, really soon?

Val wipes her mouth with a towel and bounces back into the bedroom, she feels like a giddy teenager. She jumps onto the bed and straddles him, kisses him on the mouth.

Definitely. And if you don't show up to my Halloween party, it's over.

Never.

She smiles.

I'll get fired if I miss that shift.

She hits him again with a pillow, lets him grab her waist again and throw her down into the mattress, ignores the thrum of her phone vibrating across the room as this magnificent man creates a symphony of sensations inside of her.

29

OCTOBER 25TH 2019 / LIVERPOOL

GROUP CHAT: SPOOKY GALS ☺ <3

ERICA: Val?

ERICA: Vaaaaaaaal? Where are you?! You haven't updated your socials in three straight days and I'm beginning to worry that you are in fact dead.

JOY: must still be with the new man.

ERICA: new man?

Joy's heart leaps at being addressed directly by Erica. Must play it cool.

JOY: yeh, some barman from the Pen Factory, unless he's murdered her, I'd say she's just busy getting shagged silly.

ERICA: it's alright for some, ay.

JOY: absolutely.

VAL: I'm alive!!! And yes, you are correct, I can barely walk.

JOY: ah, the throes of young love.

VAL: I'm two months older than you.

JOY: yeah yeah. How's it going with him?! Tell us everything.

VAL: short version; met at the bar, ate, drank, shagged, repeat for three whole days, he's for sure my husband.

ERICA: gross but adorable. We gonna meet him at the party?

VAL: he works there so yes!

JOY: can't wait.

VAL: gotta go, soooo much to do. X

Joy watches Val's little icon go offline, Joy takes the plunge and clicks on Erica's name.

I'm sorry, can we talk?

As soon as she sends it, a message comes through from Erica.

Can we talk? This is dumb.

Joy laughs, their timing, for the first time, impeccable.

•

Across the city, Erica smiles at her phone screen. Frankie looks up from slicing lemons in the kitchen.

Who's that, babe?

Oh, nobody.

Oooh, a surprise, is it?

Frankie's eyes light up. She hasn't stopped with the proposal excitement since Margaret mentioned it weeks ago. Every time Erica is on her phone, she is convinced it's a diamond ring conspiracy.

Ah, it's just Joy actually, babe.

Frankie puts the knife down loudly on the counter.

I thought you two weren't speaking?

Well, we weren't, but now we are. Does it matter?

It does actually yeh. This is the longest since she got back to Liverpool that you've gone without saying her name. I thought you'd focus on me a little more, but you've just been moody.

We're just friends, Erica says as she continues to tap on her phone screen.

Frankie scoffs, pours boiling water over her lemons.

I'm going to yoga.

Cool, have fun, babe.

Frankie watches as Erica stays engrossed in her phone, wondering why she is bothering to hang around waiting for a proposal from somebody who clearly doesn't intend on giving her one.

She looks at their couple costumes hanging on the door, takes a deep breath. She is probably overreacting. She leaves the flat for yoga and tries to ignore the swelling feeling of doubt in her stomach.

FACEBOOK CHAT

JOY: yeah, I know, it was just stupid.

ERICA: definitely, too much wine, we were both being daft.

JOY: absolutely.

ERICA: so, we're good?

JOY: definitely.

ERICA: phew. So, what's your costume?

JOY: still a surprise, actually.

ERICA: hmm, very curious. What about Seb? Did you get to choose his too?

JOY: HA! Yeah right. He's going as a surgeon.

ERICA: ...but he is a surgeon?

JOY: don't even start. I know. Something odd happened with him the other night too. He said he went for dinner alone, and then got really weird when I said Val was on a date.

ERICA: huh. Did they have plans?

JOY: no idea, if they did then I haven't heard about them.

ERICA: have you asked her about it?

JOY: nah, she's in this love bubble. Dinner isn't a big deal if that's what was up, he just seemed... odd about it.

ERICA: ask him about it?

JOY: hahaha, sure. Hey hubby, are you like, in love with our best mate or something? He'd love that. please, he'd boot me out and me and Bernie would have to do tricks on the street for loose change.

ERICA: you think he has feelings for her?

JOY: no, of course not. No. omg I didn't even ask what your costume is?!

ERICA: uhhhhh, God.

JOY: is it really that horrendous? What is it? a couple's costume?

ERICA: it is indeed.

JOY: oh my god, please tell me it's not something tacky like Woody and Buzz?

ERICA: HA! Imagine. I think I'd actually prefer that to what we've got.

JOY: oh, come on, you have to tell me now! It can't be any worse than those idiots that wear salt and pepper shaker costumes.

ERICA: true haha.

JOY: or the endless number of absolute tits pretending to be the joker and Harley Quinn.

ERICA: ...

JOY: stop it... really?

ERICA: she saw the film, and she just really wanted to wear the costume, and she's already blonde so the pigtails are easy apparently...

JOY: : she's made you the joker, hasn't she?

JOY: oh my god.

JOY: this is amazing.

ERICA: shut up.

JOY: are you spraying your hair green and everything?

ERICA: shut uuuuuuuup.

JOY: hahahahahahahaahahaha.

ERICA: hate you hate you hate you.

JOY: as if.

30

9AM, OCTOBER 31ST 2019 / LIVERPOOL

Joy wakes early and surveys the man lying beside her. Her husband has barely aged over the years that they have been together. The small wrinkles forming around his mouth and eyes only serving to make him more distinguished, adding more character to his sculpted face. His hair has stayed luscious, thick and dark, he is often the envy of the men at his practice, those cursed with their receding hairlines and badly covered greys. She thinks that it is unfair how men are just allowed to age naturally, whilst women are forced to cling to their youth for fear of being kicked to the curb.

She knows that around his work, women are jealous of her. They see him as a prize man, the ultimate husband. He works hard so that she can stay home, and it's been that way since she moved to London for him after university. Sure, she dabbled in some freelance stuff, but in the end, the city was too full, too competitive, she didn't have it in her. When bouts of depression and anxiety became more frequent, she stopped altogether, Seb was happy to have a stay-at-home wife. She was appreciative at the time, grateful for the break, acknowledged what a huge privilege that was. She didn't come from money, the lifestyle was new to her, almost jarring, but she settled into it.

She hired decorators for their home, took care of the food shopping, trained the dog, learnt how to cook, hosted endless dinners for his friends and colleagues or those he needed to impress. She had learnt how to put on a show, be the good wife, doting and kind, always an excellent hostess. The decay was happening beneath the surface, eating away at her in ways nobody else seemed to notice. She realised after a couple of years of that life, that she didn't have anyone besides Seb. Old friends were gone or far away, distant both physically and emotionally, her family, or what she had of it, no longer in her life. Sometimes she considered calling her dad, but memories of every other visit stopped her. It was too painful to watch him drink himself to death with a stream of destructive girlfriends by his side.

Those women who envy her do have some good points; she thinks. Here beside her is her good looking, wealthy, talented husband. He takes care of them both, provides everything they need, has endured countless bouts of her declining mental health. These things are true. But so are his secrets.

It is of no shock to Joy that she only knows half of this man. She can see it in his eyes sometimes, when they are out at dinner, or with his friends, or making love. He isn't all the way there, always somewhere else, always, she assumes, someone else's. She has of course never questioned his fidelity, not to his face. Couldn't risk losing everything, despite her hatred of it all. His secrets sit there, in a place that he thinks is all the way hidden, but she can see their edges. It wasn't until they got back to Liverpool that she realised those secrets could involve someone she knows, loves, holds dear.

Seb stirs and stretches his long legs out under the duvet. She hears the familiar click of his right knee, never quite set right after a rugby accident during his uni days. He opens his eyes, those eyes that she has looked into for the last seven years, and sighs.

Good morning to you too, she says.

Uh, he groans, do we need the sarcasm the second we wake up? Could it not wait until I've had a coffee?

Hmm, maybe, since you asked so nicely.

He pulls a half smile and swings his legs out of bed.

Have you spoken to Val? She asks him.

What?

What?

Why would you ask that?

Erm… because you're friends? It's her party tonight?

He clears the suspicion off of his face and switches to his regular charm offensive.

Of course, no, I've not heard from her.

She's busy with that new guy, I think.

Seb nods his head whilst searching the floor for his lounge pants.

I folded them up, Joy points to the corner chair on which his fleecy green comfies lie, having perfected the art of knowing what he needs without him having to verbalise it.

Oh, thanks.

He pulls them on quickly before surveying the room.

We should pack today.

You think? Can it not wait until tomorrow?

I'd like to leave as early as possible in the morning, so, no.

Right. And you're sure your mum will be okay?

She says so, not like she's dying, is it?

No, no I suppose not.

So, packing?

Oh, yep, I'll have a coffee and get onto it. You're off work today, right?

I am, but I've got a few loose ends I need to tie up here before we go home.

Right.

What?

Nothing.

He ruffles his dark hair between his fingers and throws on a t shirt.

I'll shower and come downstairs, you wanna make coffee?

Sure.

With that, he disappears into the hallway towards the

bathroom, and Joy is once again alone.

London. Tomorrow. Back home. She lets the words roll around her brain, but they don't seem real. That isn't home. She isn't even sure if Liverpool is home. As she considers getting her phone out and booking a one-way ticket to anywhere, Bernie bounces onto the bed to let her know that he needs to go outside. She kisses his wet nose and pulls her dressing gown around her.

As she goes to leave the room, she notices that Seb left his phone behind. She can't help herself. She glances round the doorway, the shower is turned on, she can hear it. His passcode is unknown to her, but she taps the screen anyway.

Instagram: @IslingtonAseteticSurgery tagged you in a post!

Facebook: It's John Stewart's birthday, let them know you're thinking of them!

Instagram: @RodneyStreetAesthetics commented on your post!

WhatsApp: Message from V.

Joy stares at the last notification. It came through at 2:11am. Weird. She checks her own phone, nothing from Val at all last night. She had assumed that she'd be shacked up with her new guy.

A strange rage surges through her, what the fuck are they doing? She picks up his phone and taps in a random combination of numbers, nothing. She knows that there are only a finite number of attempts until the phone is locked. Think, think, think.

She taps in her birthday, their wedding date, his mum's birthday. Nothing. One left, she tells herself. She knows this, she must do. She thinks back over all of their important dates, would he use any of those? He's not a 1234 man, but he would end up forgetting something complicated. Come on, Joy. Bernie barks from the doorway, trying to give her away. The phone vibrates in her hand, a message from Jason, probably some horrendously offensive meme he's found on the dark corners of Facebook. She has not missed that man this month.

Then, she has it. She bites her lip as she types it in.

6969.

The phone vibrates again, nope. Damn, she thinks, she was sure of that one.

She hears the shower turn off and returns the phone to where it was, tries to ignore the feeling in her stomach. She gathers herself and follows Bernie out of the room, the anxious nausea building inside of her. As she gets to the back door to let him out, she can't hold it in anymore. She runs to the kitchen sink and throws up into it, the undigested bits of last night's dinner hitting the Belfast porcelain. She wipes her mouth and turns on the tap, drinks from it, cleans the sink out.

Well, Margaret's voice comes from the doorway.

Shit, Margaret, I'm sorry, I've cleaned it. I'm not sick, honestly, it's just anxiety.

Mm, I remember when I had that type of anxiety, nine months later our Seb popped out.

Joy stares dumbly at her mother-in-law.

What?

Pregnant, dear. I recognise the look on your face, sickly, tired, a bit bloated.

I'm just stressed out, it happens sometimes, but cheers for the concern.

If you say so, dear.

Joy shudders and heads outside to the garden, lets the fierce morning wind hit her face, blow the cobwebs away.

Pregnant? The thought makes her skin crawl. It may be the most natural thing in the world, but all she can picture is that one scene from Alien. Her phone pings in her pocket, she gets it out in a daze.

Erica.

Can't wait to see you later, sorry if that's weird, but it's true. Happy Halloween x

She smiles at the screen, wants nothing more than to see Erica, hold her, kiss her, hide underneath a duvet with her and let everything else just melt away.

Joy?

Seb's voice from the door startles her.

I'm heading out, I'll be back in time to get ready for the party.

Joy just nods, doesn't bother asking where he is going, isn't entirely sure she cares.

He does an awkward wave, and leaves. Joy watches numbly as Bernie digs a hole in the garden and buries one of Margaret's weird gnomes in it.

She pats her leg and he happily runs to her, following her into the kitchen, treading his muddy paws onto the spotless floor.

31

10:30AM. OCTOBER 31ST 2019 / LIVERPOOL

She knows it's him before she even answers the intercom. Three sharp presses of the button, the metallic buzz sending shockwaves through her living room, settling deep in her stomach. She knew he would turn up at some point, that he wouldn't be able to resist coming here before he and Joy leave tomorrow, try and claw her back to him.

She has felt bad the last few days, seeing his endless messages come through, all without a response. She had hoped that he would just stop trying, leave her alone, go back to London. Leave all the painful things to say left unsaid, bury it all deep.

The buzzer goes again.

Guess not, she thinks.

With a deep breath, she brings her finger to the button of the speaker, plays dumb.

Hello?

Val, let me in.

Seb?

Val!

I don't know if it's a great idea you being here, Seb.

Why? Is *he* in there?

No-no, it's just-

So, it's true! My god, V, you could have told me.

Look, Seb, it's not that simple, I-

Please, just let me up, please baby, I need to see you.

Seb-

Please? I'm begging you V; I just need to see you.

She feels herself relent, disappointed in her own finger as it reaches to the 'enter' button and presses gingerly. She always gives into him. Always.

She bites the skin around her manicured thumbnail as she paces her hallway, waiting for him. Jack had left the evening before for work, all giddy kisses and exhausted limbs. She wishes now that he was here, that she didn't have to do this.

The door opens and he steps inside, his face hollow, pale. He stands in place, shrugs his coat off, places it on the hooks next to him.

Seb, I know I should have told you.

Yeah, yeah, you should have.

He is quiet, shrunken, she hasn't seen him like this before, usually so assertive, dominant.

The text I sent last night, I know it may have seemed a little abrupt, it's just-

It's time we drew a line under this, I'm sorry?

Val looks at the floor.

You thought that what? I was going to read that, agree, and fuck off back to London never to think of you again?

No, I don't know.

He walks towards her then, reaches out to touch her arm, the warm grip of his hand familiar on her soft skin.

V, look at me, please.

He touches her chin with his fingers, lifts her face up to meet his. Her eyes are shimmering, threatening tears. His hand gently moves to her cheek.

I can't lose you.

Seb, you're not mine. I need something else, something more. I don't think you know how much it hurts me every time you leave, every time you go back to a home without me.

Then fine. Be mine. I'll tell Joy as soon as I can, today, even. Then it's just me and you, okay? That's what you want, right?

Val feels the world drop within her solar plexus. The words she has wanted to hear for the best part of a decade finally tumbling out of his beautiful mouth. She cannot form a response.

He pulls her closer to him, slips his free hand around her waist, and kisses her softly.

I love you, V.

Tears come then, and despite everything in her body responding to his kiss, his words, she pushes her hands against his chest, parts her lips from his.

Seb, I can't. I've wanted to hear you say that for longer than you'll ever know. But you've waited until you're losing me to say it.

She shakes her head.

This thing, this mess that we have, it's gone on too long, hurt me too much. I just can't do it anymore. I can't do it to Joy, or to myself.

You've been doing it to Joy for years, V.

His shift in tone startles her.

I could tell her, he says, I could tell her everything. And then what, V? We'd be free to be together.

I'm just not… I'm not sure I want that anymore.

Right, he laughs, wiping his lips with the back of his hand.

It's been so good-

Don't fucking humour me. It's this new guy, isn't it? Must be something real special, ay?

It's not just him, Seb, it's everything, all of it. I just can't do it, not anymore. It's not good for us. For anyone.

What if I just tell her, hm? What then? I could *ruin* you, V. Fucking ruin you.

Val's heart races in her chest as she tries to compose herself. He reaches out to touch her again.

But it doesn't have to be like that, baby, just see sense. It's me

and you. We can go get lunch, maybe a nice hotel again? Have some drinks, get back to normal-

Normal?! Seb, none of this is, or ever has been fucking *normal.* You're married. To my best friend. That fact hasn't changed, and yeah, that makes me a rotten person too, but I'd never try and blackmail you with it. So, you know what, *baby*, if you wanna ruin me, go ahead. I can't do this anymore.

V, no, come on I-

Get the fuck out of my apartment.

Baby, he says softly, reaching towards her again.

Don't you dare fucking touch me, Seb. Get out. Go home, to your wife, where you've always gone. This is over.

He takes a breath to speak again, but he thinks better of it.

Fine. See you at the party.

With that, he grabs his coat and slams her door behind him.

Shit, Val thinks, *the party.*

She drops onto her sofa, pulls a blanket over her legs, and waits for the tears to come.

Nothing.

Her phone buzzes then, a text from Jack.

Hey you, shift doesn't start till 5; wanna hang out this afternoon? Lunch and an orgasm on me?

She laughs at the screen, all of the horror of the last ten minutes quickly melting from her. She can't think about Seb anymore, he's not hers.

He never was.

32

11AM. OCTOBER 31ST 2019 / LIVERPOOL

Joy unclips Bernie's lead at the gate of the park, throws his ball as far as she can and watches him chase after it with pure joy, mud flinging from all four paws. She walks slowly, letting the crisp air of the morning fill her lungs, tries to ignore the rising nausea as she thinks about going back to London tomorrow. Back to her life of mundanity, cooking, cleaning, existing. Back to her life without Erica. The thought of that makes her want to sob.

She thinks of Seb, tries to muster the same emotion at the thought of going back to a life that didn't contain him, but comes up empty.

But what if you're pregnant?

The thought pushes its way into her head before she can stop it. She tries to brush it off. Anxiety has always messed with her insides, come out in gross physical ways, she tells herself that this is no different. She hasn't been on the pill in two years, came off it when she thought it might be making her depressive episodes worse, never went back on it when she and Seb stopped having regular sex. She tries to pull back the hazy memories of that night a few weeks ago, when they first got to Liverpool, drunken giggles and fumbling hands. She curses herself for not being more careful, for not remembering if they were or not. She knows she needs to take a test, but the thought of returning to her life in London with Seb and also a baby on the way makes her want to rip her own skin off.

She pulls a pack of Marlboro's from her coat pocket, fumbles around for her ancient lighter, tries it a few times, nothing. She tries again, shielding her face from the wind, but again, nothing. Once more, she places her thumb at the top of the small metal wheel and strikes it down, this time, it sticks completely. Broken.

Joy lets out a small, incredulous laugh. Finally, it's packed in. After all these years. She pulls out her phone, finds Erica's name, and clicks on it. Usually, the thought of phone calls would make her sick with nerves, not right now. It only rings once.

Hello?

Hey.

You alright? We don't do real life phone calls, are you dying?

Ha, no, but the lighter is. Has. The lighter's died, is what I called to say.

What?! Finally?!

Finally.

Spooky that it's happened on Halloween.

I knew you'd say that.

It *is* spooky though! You obviously think so to, otherwise you wouldn't have called me.

Can't argue there.

Where are you?

Park with Bernie, freezing my tits off.

I could totally make a gross joke somehow right now, but I'll spare you.

Mm, how considerate, what a gentleman.

You should give it a burial.

I'm not insane.

Hey, that lighter has been through some shit, it needs a proper send off.

Well, maybe we can toss it into the Mersey together tonight or something, a Viking funeral but like… scouse.

Toss me in there too before I have to put this sodding costume on.

Oh my god, you have absolutely no idea how excited I am to see it.

Stop it.

I've just always thought you had joker energy; you know?

Stop iiiiit.

Not that anything could ever beat the Ziggy Stardust costume.

I'm literally a puddle of embarrassment right now.

Don't be, I loved that costume.

Sure you did.

I did! Not sure how well you remember, but I got off with you whilst you were wearing it. There were wig bits in my mouth and everything.

Such a romantic time.

I can't believe you showed up wearing that, such balls on you.

I thought it was going to be a costume party! Who hosts a Halloween party without a strict fancy dress code?

Fair point. I'm glad though. Might not have found you if you weren't dressed like a shiny red disco ball.

Found me?

Yeah, found you.

You were looking for me that night?

Of course. I know we'd only met for like five seconds a few days before in that horrid little college smoking area, but I wanted to see you again.

You did?

Yeah, you were dead fit.

Dickhead.

True though.

That's so weird. I only went to that party to see if you'd be there.

Silence down the phone.

Really?

Yeah, I dragged my friends there and everything, both of whom have babies and weirdly identical husbands now, by the way.

Why did we never tell each other this back then?

I dunno, trying to stay aloof and cool, I guess.

Christ, we were idiots.

We still are, arguably.

Mm.

A bark from Bernie brings Joy back to the present, he bounds towards her and flops to the ground, exposing his belly, thick with mud, for a scratch. She apologises to him for the lack of fusses and hooks his lead back to his harness and they continue their walk.

You're out with Bernie?

Yeah, needed some air.

In Formby?

Yeah, why?

Do you… are you around for coffee, or something?

Oh, erm…

Don't worry if not, it's fine, I know you're busy with stuff and-

No, no, I can, I want to.

I just thought I could hop on the train maybe and- but if you can't it's totally fine and-

E, yes, get on the train.

Joy can hear the smile on Erica's face as they agree a meeting place, she tries to keep her voice cool as they cut the call off. She looks at Bernie, muddy and panting.

Change of plan, buddy.

She leads them towards the exit of the park, trying not to walk as fast as she would like to, not to let the manic grin creep over her face as she all but drags Bernie towards the high street.

*

Joy settles outside of a café promoting the World's Best Coffee with Bernie at her feet, eyes scanning the street for a familiar pop of orange hair. A teenage waitress donning a huge cardigan and a lot of eye makeup pops her head out of the door, not wanting to come out into the cold.

What's yours, love?

Oh, I'm just waiting for a friend, I'll order when she gets here.

With a suspicious eye at the dog and a pop of her gum, she disappears back inside. Joy waits, tries not to look like she is doing so. She gets out her phone, scrolls without really taking anything in. Somebody's having a baby, somebody's dead, somebody's stabbed someone else in central London, somebody's raising money for their cat's surgery. Out of habit, she finds Erica's profile and looks at the picture. Bright hair, bright smile, bright eyes. She feels a surge of affection towards this woman that she has known for so long, this woman that she let go, feels the familiar ache in her chest starting to form when she is interrupted by Bernie standing to attention.

Joy looks up, and there she is. Perfection in an oversized hoody, immediately leaning down to fuss the dog, letting him lick her hands. Joy quickly clicks the sleep button on the side of her phone and puts it face down on the cold metal table in front of her.

Hey, Erica smiles as she pulls Joy into her for a hug.

Joy muffles a greeting back as she holds Erica close to her, perhaps for a second longer than is necessary.

Did you order?

No, waited for you.

Such a gent.

Always.

So, Erica says as she slips into the seat next to Joy, dreading tonight?

Not quite as much as you, I don't think.

Fair enough. I'm not sure I'll ever forgive Val for not letting go of the costume rule.

Joy lets out a small laugh, nods, looks down at the table.

You alright? You seem… down?

No, I'm fine, it's just cold.

Joy clasps her hands together, blows on them. Erica reaches across the table and takes them in hers, rubs them quickly to warm them up.

That better? She asks, not letting go.

Joy can only muster a nod as she feels her stomach hitting the floor at this direct contact, feels as though she might break inside if Erica were to let go.

The door to the café dings, and the waitress pops her head back out. Erica pulls her hands away quickly. Joy wants to scream.

What're you having, then?

Two lattes with oat milk, and a bowl of water for the dog, please, Erica says.

The waitress rolls her eyes and disappears again, the 'no dogs allowed indoors' sign hitting against the door as it closes.

Charming, deffo a big tip for her.

Joy laughs, lightly hits Erica's hand with hers, wants so much to leave it there, to be touching her again.

So… you're really leaving tomorrow then?

Joy tries to keep herself composed as she nods in response.

Maybe I could come and visit, or something?

Oh, yeah, I'm sure Frankie would just *love* that.

I just don't want you to go back there and disappear again, you know? Like, I feel like I've just gotten you back and now…

I know.

Do you?

Of course.

So why do it then? Correct me if I'm wrong but you don't seem exactly thrilled to be going back to London.

I'm not, but it's not that easy.

Why not, Joy? If you're unhappy there, stay here.

And do what, E? I don't have a job, I don't have anywhere to live, anywhere to go. I don't have money of my own, the last few years of my life have just been me existing inside of somebody else's life and letting mine revolve around that.

So, you're just going to go back to London and live a life that you hate because it's too hard to do anything else?

Don't say it like that, fucking hell.

I'm sorry but that's just what it seems like you're doing. You could find something to do here, some bar job, anything, you could make it work.

I'm *married.*

Silence from Erica.

What? You have a big opinion about that, too?

Does he make you happy?

How can you-

Joy, really. Does he? Are you happy?

Joy looks down at the metal table, fights back the tears that are threatening hotly at her eyes. This isn't the flirty coffee chat that she was expecting.

I don't know anymore.

Joy, I-

The door opens, the waitress returning with two steaming cups of coffee on a tray. She sets them down carefully, somehow missing the thick air, the rising tension, the strained silence.

That's nine pounds eighty, she says, holding out the card machine.

Joy picks up her phone and double clicks the button, waits for the familiar beep of Apple Pay.

Thanks, the waitress mutters as she returns to the warmth of indoors.

Joy wraps her hands around the mug, let's the heat seep through to her skin, her throat feels tight, she doesn't want to sit and drink coffee like things are normal.

Can we walk?

Erica doesn't object, just takes three big gulps out of her mug, stashes the fancy biscuit in her pocket and gets up. Joy follows,

Bernie walking by her side, the tiring morning having turned him into a Very Good Boy.

They walk in silence, each of them afraid to break it, afraid of what may tumble out of their mouths, unable to put back in.

After ten minutes of agonizing silence, Erica pulls her phone out, checks the time.

It's midday, she says.

Yeah?

Acceptable drinking hour, and there's a pub right up ahead.

The corner of Joy's mouth creeps upwards, and her mood lifts immediately with the look of mischief on Erica's face.

She nods, and they speed walk to the small pub, the warmth of a freshly lit fire hitting them as soon as they open the large wooden door. Joy leads Bernie to a table in the corner where the heat from the flames can be felt, while Erica disappears to the bar to quickly return with a pint of cider in each hand, and a bag of crisps hanging from between her teeth.

They clink glasses, take a large sip each.

God that's so much better than coff-

I love you.

Joy splutters and coughs in response. Erica doesn't break eye contact.

You… E-

I can't not say it anymore, Joy. I loved you when I met you, I loved you ever since, I'm so fucking tired of not saying it, so, fuck it. I fucking love you.

Joy watches as relief floods Erica's face at the words finally being released, escaping into the space between them, the tension visibly leaving her shoulders.

I don't expect you to say anything, I know things are-

I love you too.

Erica bites her lip, her eyes brimming with hot tears.

You do?

Of course I fucking do.

And, just like that, the drinks are left on the table in front of them, condensation dripping down the sides of the cold glasses, as Joy and Erica's lips touch for the first time in years. Gentle at first, and then hungrier, as they pull each other closer together, Joy's hand cupping Erica's face, Erica's hand gripping the small of Joy's back. Seconds that feel like minutes go by, when they pull apart slightly, foreheads touching, delirious smiles.

Fuck, Joy whispers, laughing.

I missed you, Erica whispers back.

Joy moves her hand, wipes a tear from Erica's flushed face, kisses her on the tip of her pixie-like nose.

Never again, she says, as they hug each other tightly, laughing and trying to shake off the shock of what just happened. They both pick up their pint glasses, clink them together and take a sip, their free hands woven together, tightly.

A sigh of relief and then,

We need to tell them.

33

2PM. OCTOBER 31ST 2019 / LIVERPOOL

Joy walks home in a daze, a giddy smile on her face that refuses to budge, despite the rising dread inside of her as she approaches Margaret's house. The past hour had been a blur of Erica, a delirious fever dream of everything she had wanted for the best part of a decade.

She needs to talk to Seb, explain everything, deal with the repercussions of what happened, how she feels, how she's been feeling, how she is leaving. A text comes through from Val as she nears the front door.

> SO excited for tonight! Get there early so we can have a head start on shots. LY xo

Shit, Joy thinks, the party.

She can't ruin Val's night, not after all the hard work she has put into it, how much she's been looking forward to it. If they don't turn up, Val will be hurt. If they do turn up and make a scene, Val will be hurt. Entertained, perhaps, but hurt all the same. Maybe she should wait until after the party, but the thought of keeping these words trapped inside of her for any longer makes her want to scream.

She unhooks Bernie's lead at the front door and lets him into the house, the smell of coffee wafting through the hallway.

Hello?

In here, Seb shouts from the kitchen.

Joy pulls off her gloves and steels herself, whatever happens today will be worth it. She opens the door to see Seb sitting at the island, a small bouquet of roses and two coffees in front of him.

What's this?

I just thought, well, I wanted to say thank you, for being so great while we've been here, I know it stresses you out, and I appreciate it.

Joy eyes the coffee cups warily, trying to scramble back in her memory banks for the last time that Seb did anything even vaguely romantic for her.

He pushes one of the mugs towards her.

Almond milk, I remembered.

Joy smiles weakly, picks the mug up and sips at it, trying to form a thought, a word, anything.

Anyway, he continues, oblivious to her inner turmoil, we'll be home tomorrow, and I can't wait.

He stands up, leans over to kiss her forehead, his large hand on her back feels foreign, it doesn't belong there, she wonders if it ever did. As she takes a breath to verbalise the thought, he interrupts her.

So, the plan. I thought we could pack up now, get ready, and then go get some drinks together before the party? It's been ages since we've done anything like that, hasn't it?

It has, yeah.

Great!

He seems jubilant with his ability to make a plan that she doesn't hate, suddenly playing the role of caring husband. He leans towards her then, tries to kiss her mouth, but she flinches slightly, some irrational voice in her brain telling her that he will erase Erica with his lips. It doesn't faze him. He picks up his coffee and hums a tune as he leaves the room, on his way upstairs to do his version of packing, which Joy has historically had to redo throughout their entire relationship.

She sits at the island, letting the heat from the mug keep her grounded to the room, the house, this place, this marriage, this man. She feels the familiar panic rise in her stomach, her heart beginning to pound irregularly, a cold sweat forming on her brow. She takes a deep breath, squeezes her eyes shut, forces herself to focus on the heat of the mug, the feel of her toes in her socks, anything to ground her, to stop herself from spiralling.

She releases the mug and fumbles around in her pocket for cigarettes, her fingers finding the broken smiley face lighter, battered, old, useless now, she grips it tightly, thinks of Erica, of her lips, her hair, her smile, her laugh, that one weirdly long hair that insists on growing from her arm, and feels her breath return to normal. Nausea rises and fades in the rhythm she has become so familiar with over the years, she rides the wave of it, ignores the bleating voice in her head that is shouting for her to take a pregnancy test, because then what? Then what happens? She can't think about it.

She stands up and steadies herself on the kitchen island, puts a cigarette between her teeth. She clicks a ring of the range cooker on, leans into it to light the tip, and lets herself into the garden. Margaret will fume about the smell of smoke in the kitchen later on.

Joy looks out at the garden, frost melting and leaving behind ugly muddy clumps in its place.

She lets herself look at the fork in the road ahead of her, wonders which path she is going to end up taking, hopes that she has a choice in the matter.

34

4PM. OCTOBER 31ST 2019 / LIVERPOOL

Frankie leans over the bathroom sink, carefully spraying the ends of her ponytails, one blue, one pink. She surveys herself in the small mirror, and lets out an excited shriek.

How're you getting along in there, babe? She shouts through to the bedroom.

Oh, yep, fine.

Erica sits distractedly at the vanity, trying loosely to focus on applying face paint whilst also trying to come up with a way to nicely dump her girlfriend before the party. Frankie totters into the bedroom, does a spin to show Erica her full outfit.

Soooooo, what do you think?

Lovely, Franks, really nice.

I think I'd have made a great Harley Quinn, although I was never very good as gymnastics in school. Do you think if I were Harley Quinn, I'd have to know how to do a forward roll? I could never really get the hang of it, and I feel like she might-

Frankie, we need to talk.

Erica gestures for her to sit down on the bed.

Look, the past year, it's been great, I just, things are-

It's Joy, isn't it?

Erica looks at her then, startled, her big blue eyes shimmering with held back tears behind her carefully applied Harley makeup. Erica doesn't respond. Frankie nods slowly.

I'm not stupid, Erica, despite what people think.

I don't think you are.

You've been treating me like you do. You think I haven't noticed the change in you the last month? Imagine having to watch your girlfriend light up at the mere mention of another woman's name, let alone have to sit in her fucking house with her fuckboy of a husband and force down food she's made you while you talk to her stupid fancy fucking mother-in-law and all the while your girlfriend is…

The rest becomes indecipherable as she descends into tears, pulling her legs into herself and sobbing into her knees. Erica reaches out to comfort her, but Frankie pulls her shoulder away. It is then that Erica realises that she and Joy didn't think about this bit, the other people, the lives they'd be changing after making this decision for themselves. Frankie doesn't deserve this.

She watches as Frankie unfurls herself, wiping her eyes with the back of her hand.

Inappropriate time, I know, Erica ventures, but… your angry Harley Quinn makeup actually looks really good now.

Frankie lets out a laugh, tears still rolling down her cheeks, as she reaches for a pillow behind her and hits Erica with it.

I'm sorry, Franks, I am, I know it's a horrendous cliché, I hate myself for saying it, but it's really not you.

I know, she says, it's Joy.

She looks sad then, stares down at the carpet, sniffling.

Look, we can still go to the party, if you want. You put so much effort into the costume.

I wasn't going to *not* go, its Val's party, as if I'd miss it just because my girlfriend is in love with someone else. Lame.

Erica smiles then, reaches out to take her hand, Frankie lets her.

Really, Franks, I am sorry.

I know, me too. It would have never worked out anyways, I couldn't spend my life with somebody who isn't deeply invested in Taylor Swift's discography.

Frankie takes a deep, shaky breath, and Erica squeezes her hand.

Come on, Erica says, let's get a gin in you.

Okay, Frankie musters a smile.

They both stand to leave the room, before Erica remembers.

Just one thing, a minute ago, you said that Joy's husband is a fuckboy. Why is that? Is that just something we call men now?

Frankie is silent for a moment, and then shrugs her shoulders.

Fuck it, not my problem anymore, I guess. I saw him and Val together.

What, like in a bar?

Yeah.

So? They're friends, right?

Mm, he wasn't looking at her like they are friends, wasn't touching her like they are friends.

You think there's something going on between them?

Does it matter? You're trying to steal his wife anyways.

With that, Frankie leaves the room, and Erica hears her rustling around in the fridge to assemble a gin and tonic as she sits back on the bed, digesting what Frankie just told her.

Val and Seb?

Val and Seb?!

She gets out her phone instinctively to call Joy but thinks better of it. They will see each other in a few hours, she may have even broken it off with him by then, there will be time to tell her this.

Another time.

35

6PM. OCTOBER 31ST 2019 / LIVERPOOL

Pride and excitement rush through Valencia as she turns on the lights for the party. The whole room filled with Halloween decorations, candles, fairy lights, a cute little projector casting black and green sheet ghosts onto the ceiling. She surveys the buffet table, ensures that things are clearly labelled vegan and gluten free. She sneaks a sausage roll from under one of the lids and pops it into her mouth, heaven.

From behind the bar, she sees Jack busily pouring entrance bubbles for her guests, his body language relaxed and happy as he jokes with the barman next to him. He looks up and catches her eye. She blushes immediately, fanning her oversized eyelashes in his direction, she mouths a 'meow', apt in her cat costume. He laughs, thank God, as she may have melted into the floor if not.

Val checks her phone; people should be arriving any minute now. She opens up Instagram and takes a quick picture of herself, blurry enough to satisfy her Gen Z audience but chic enough to appeal to the millennials. She slides her phone into her bag, vowing not to look at it unless to take pictures, to resist the urge to read the replies, the comments.

The playlist starts, a compilation of party music to ease everybody into it, before the cheesy Halloween hits come out later on, when people are drunk enough to do the Monster Mash. She sits on a stool at the bar, takes one of the flutes of prosecco and sips at it. Jack, like a magnet, is by her side immediately.

Excited?

Nervous.

You do this every year, no?

Still, nervous.

I am too, a bit.

You? Why?

Your friends might not like me.

Ha, sure.

No, you're right, I'm brilliant.

Val narrows her eyes, mimes being sick.

Prettiest cat I've ever seen, he says as he kisses her briefly on the lips and returns to his post behind the bar. Val lets the butterflies and prosecco warm her soul, enjoying the moment to herself before people start arriving.

As she finishes the glass, she hears the door open.

Vaaaaaal, Joy exclaims, her arms outstretched for a hug.

She wraps her arms around Joy, trying desperately to avoid eye contact with Seb as she does so. Joy finally lets her go, leaving her to greet him.

Seb, thanks for coming, I know you hate these things.

Anything for you, he says with a comedic bow, and pulls her in for a hug. She pulls away from him after a beat, doesn't want him to get the wrong idea.

You guys look amazing, Val says, holding one of Joy's hands as she twirls around in a sweeping black dress, wig to match.

Morticia is an icon, you do her justice.

Thanks, V.

And you, she turns to Seb, such a feat of the imagination, how on earth did you come up with it?

He blushes under her attention in his green surgical scrubs.

What can I say, I inspire myself.

I can see that, she says, punching his arm playfully. How quickly she can slip back into this role with him. She shakes it off.

So, bubbles are here, help yourselves.

Val gestures to the glasses behind her as she sees another group of people entering.

I'll catch up with you guys later, okay? Gotta go play hostess.

She leaves them both by the bar to greet her guests, fully in her element as she compliments costumes, laughs at jokes and directs people towards the alcohol.

She looks great, hey? Says Joy, watching as Val reveals her perfect teeth for a selfie with somebody at the door.

Mm, Seb mumbles, draining a glass of prosecco. He puts the empty glass back on the bar and tries to get the attention of a barman, who gestures that he will be one minute.

You've been quiet today, he says.

Yeah, I dunno, I'm not really feeling myself.

You'll feel better when we're back in London.

Yeah, about that, I'm not really-

Double whiskey and coke, mate, and a wine for the wife.

Which wine? The barman asks.

I dunno, Seb replies, he turns to Joy, gestures for her to tell him.

Sauvignon, please, thank you.

The barman nods, turns away to make their drinks.

You still don't know which wine I like? After all these years?

It's not a big deal, Joy, he says as he hands a twenty over the bar.

She feels everything that she wants to say bubble up inside of her, but now is not the time, here is not the place. Instead, she puts on a smile and takes a large gulp of her drink.

I'm going for a smoke.

Fine.

Seb turns to lean on the bar, sips at his drink. Joy feels nothing.

36

7:39PM. OCTOBER 31ST 2019 / LIVERPOOL

Joy fiddles with a stray bit of hair from her wig as she sits on the stone steps of the beer garden. She brings the tip of her cigarette to it and lets it singe, the smell of burning plastic filling the air around her as she blows out the tiny spark. The party is in full swing, groups of Val's old friends, some that Joy knows and some she doesn't are milling around and oozing sophistication, turning their noses up at the high fat cheeses on the buffet table. Val pointed out a few different influencers that she knows through social media, who, as far as Joy has seen, have done nothing but take a few pictures and then sit alone looking at their phones.

Seb is circulating the party in that natural way that he has, charming any woman in his path with his impressive job, his sharp jawline. Joy has watched many men at parties over the years pull their girlfriends a little closer, hold their hands a little tighter, as he offers to buy the couple a drink and regales them with a funny story from his uni days.

No sign of Erica yet, she checks her phone again but is met with no notifications. She wonders if they have broken up, or if Erica got home and realised she had made a huge mistake, if she's being ghosted by the love of her life. The thought brings the nausea back.

She drains her glass and peers through the large windows into the bar, searching for that familiar pop of orange hair, some horrid polyester joker costume paired with it.

As if manifested, Erica appears in the doorway to the beer garden, holding a beer and looking exhausted. Joy's heart leaps into her throat immediately, she holds her arm up in the air to get her attention. Erica looks relieved as she spots Joy, pushes through the crowd of smokers towards her, her creepy painted joker smile getting closer.

Hi.

Hey.

Erica puts her glass down next to Joy's.

Are you… okay?

Erica nods.

I did it.

You did it?

I did it, I told her, it's over.

Wow, that's… wow.

She took it really well, to be fair, she's come here with me still.

What?

Yeah, she's in there somewhere.

Erica gestures to the packed bar.

Fuck.

I know, could definitely have been worse.

I'm glad it didn't suck for you.

Erica tilts her head; Joy tries not to think of that one scene in The Dark Knight.

You haven't done it yet, I'm guessing?

No, it just seemed like tonight-

Isn't the night, I know.

Just with Val's party and everything…

Joy, it's okay, I know.

Erica's hands find Joy's, and Joy lets out a sigh of relief at their fingers intertwine. Erica's thumb rubs her wrist.

Can't believe you never got that removed, Erica says, looking at the faded and shaky outline of a seagull on Joy's wrist.

How could I? It's all I had left of you at one point, we really should have taken more pictures together or something, do you know how hard it is to pine over someone when they never update their socials?

My apologies, Erica laughs.

And, if I remember correctly, you promised you'd have a bird tattoo for me.

I did.

And yet, here I stand, betrayed, bereft of matching bird tattoo.

Erica releases Joy's hands and starts to unbutton her jacket.

What're you doing?

Just, hang on a sec.

She takes the jacket off and reveals a tank top underneath, she pulls the straps off her shoulders, revealing a chest piece tattoo made of two detailed magpies in flight, surrounded by leaves, all in muted colours and deep shades of black. Joy's mouth drops open.

It's beautiful, she says, resisting the urge to reach out and touch it, knowing that despite the realistic feathers, it would just be Erica's warm skin under her fingers.

You like it?

I love it, magpies?

Two for Joy.

Her breath catches in her throat then, eyes brimming with tears. She can't help herself, just pulls Erica towards her and lets the familiar electricity crackle between them as they kiss, she brings a hand up to her face. Erica opens her eyes and sees the woman she loves so thoroughly, their foreheads touching, a smile on both of their faces.

Erica brings her hand up to touch Joy's, squeezes it hard.

You need to tell him.

Joy nods lightly.

I know.

I love you.

I know that, too.

37

8PM. OCTOBER 31ST 2019 / LIVERPOOL

Frankie watches from the doorway, hurt slowly being replaced by anger. Hot flashes of it surge through her body. She had been so understanding, so kind, so *pathetic* when Erica had predictably broken it off earlier, but was she now expected to look at it? To be made to look like a jilted fool in front of the entire party?

She looks on as Erica takes off her purple joker jacket and shows Joy her chest tattoo, those birds that have always terrified Frankie, no doubt some call-back to their ridiculously romanticised past. And then they are kissing. Not just drunk-at-a-party kissing, but properly kissing. Like one-of-them-has-just-returned-from-war kissing.

Frankie waits for tears, but none come. Instead, she takes a swig of her gin and asks the man next to her for a cigarette, despite never having smoked one before. This is what bitter people do, right?

Sorry love, I don't smoke.

Right, never mind then.

As she is so accustomed to, his attention doesn't leave her when she wants it to.

Here all by yourself then, are you?

Kind of.

Pretty little thing like you? Madness.

His breath smells like pickled onions, and makes Frankie think of Monster Munch. He leans in closer, turning his back on his pack of friends. They don't bat an eyelid, all used to peeling off from one another in a desperate attempt to get laid.

Actually, my regular date is over there, kissing her ex-girlfriend. She points in the direction of Erica and Joy, who are now whispering sweet stupid nothings to each other.

Woah, that's hot. Guys, he turns back to the pack, check it out.

They all turn to get a look at two women kissing that they didn't have to search on Pornhub for, making approving noises.

Well, more fool her. Listen, if you want, I could show you what you've been-

Please, don't finish that sentence.

He reels back, offended.

Fuck you, then.

You wish, she says with a well-practiced cold grin.

She slams her glass down on the table in front of her and makes for the exit, the smell of pickled onion breath haunting her as she leaves. She needs to find her coat, needs to get out of here, needs to put on her pyjamas and cry or go full Lemonade and break everything that Erica has ever touched with a bat and then go and buy a cat or a rabbit and call it her son because she will probably be alone forever.

Instead, she enters the bar and searches for the chair that she put her coat on, ignoring the hand she just felt on her behind.

Frankie! Val appears in front of her, a vision in cat ears and glittery eyeliner.

Val, hey, look I've got to go, I'm sorry, I just-

What?! But it's so early! Come on, let's do a shot, come with me.

Frankie let's herself be led to the bar and people clear a path.

This, she points a perfectly manicured hand to the handsome guy behind the bar, is Jack, and he's the world's best bartender.

She slurs her words and bats her eyes at the barman. He pours two shots of Sambuca and leans over the bar to kiss her as he hands them over.

I'm just like… assuming you know that guy, right? Frankie shouts over the music.

Yessss, yes, we're seeing each other, it's brilliant.

Oh, Frankie says, surprised.

What?

Val throws her head back and takes the shot.

What about Seb?

What about me?

Frankie turns around to see his tall frame standing behind her.

She takes the Sambuca shot, wondering how to play this out. She knows she should bow out, stop meddling, go home, have a hot bath, watch Bridget Jones, but the anger is still coursing through her veins, along with several drinks.

Just wondering how it's going to work with Val's new boyfriend, like, are you guys going to be a throuple? Or are Joy and Erica going to join in too? Like that weird cult where they all married each other, you know?

Seb switches seamlessly to amused confusion.

How much have you had to drink, love?

About the same amount I had when I saw you two out with each other a few weeks back, she smiles to him sweetly.

His face darkens, Val watches dumbstruck, a small hiccup escaping her mouth.

Have you told Joy? He asks, quietly.

Frankie shrugs in response, enjoying the feeling of being puppet master. She spots her coat on a chair behind Seb and grabs it.

You all deserve each other, she says, before turning to leave.

She cannot ignore the swell of disappointment that she feels in Val, the tragic inevitability of a bored husband, the cliché of it being somebody the wife knows and loves, the oncoming fallout leading to the happy ending of her now ex-girlfriend.

Frankie bursts out of the front door of the bar and takes a deep breath, slips on her coat, and begins the walk home through the clear Liverpool night.

She lets the familiar sounds of her entire city having a party comfort her as she walks.

38

8:30PM. OCTOBER 31ST 2019 / LIVERPOOL

Does Joy know?

Val shrugs.

V, this is serious, does Joy know?

Jesus, Seb, I have no idea. I'm assuming that if she knew we'd been fucking then she'd have maybe had something to say about it.

Fuck.

Go find her if you're that worried.

Everything okay, babe? Jack asks from behind the bar.

We're fine, thanks mate, Seb replies darkly.

I wasn't asking you, *mate.*

I'm fine, babe, it's fine.

Jack gives Seb a long look and nods, goes back to serving the bar.

Babe? Seb asks incredulously.

Val's face burns up.

That's the guy? Really? Some bartender in town? That's who you've sacked me off for?

I didn't *sack you off*, Seb, you're fucking married. To Joy. My friend, Joy.

Picked a funny time to gain a moral compass, didn't you?

Fuck you, I'm trying.

And *I'm* trying to keep my fucking life together. Where's Joy?

Val points towards the beer garden.

Seb turns to make his way out, pushing through the crowds

of people, impatience fuelling him. He gets to the doors and peers above the clusters of smokers, trying not to get burned by cigarette ends as he strains through them.

And then he sees them.

His wife and her old friend sitting next to each other on the steps. They are close together, each holding the others hand, a drink in the other. He stands back a little, observes. They have an ease, they are laughing. Joy looks happy. At that moment, Erica leans in and kisses his wife briskly on the cheek, lingering a little longer than he likes.

Joy?

Her head shoots up at the sound of her name, she immediately drops Erica's hand and stands up.

Seb, what are you- are you okay?

Fine, yes, and you?

Yep, yeah, good.

He walks towards them.

You two having fun?

Yes, lovely time.

Looks like it.

He turns to Erica.

Your girlfriend left.

Oh, did she?

Mm, I wonder what upset her so much.

She was upset?

Seemed it. Left pretty swiftly.

Well, we actually, erm, we actually split up today, so.

Ah, I see. And that's what this is, right? Joy making you feel better?

Seb, Joy warns.

No, no, let her speak, because I'd really like to know what the fuck is going on here. Are you trying it on with my wife?

Erica laughs at that.

What's so funny?

Nothing it's just that-

Sebastian?

They all turn at the sound of Margaret's voice and watch as she wheels her way through the crowd, batting people who didn't notice her with an umbrella. She, appropriately, is dressed as Cruella De Ville.

Sorry I'm late, darlings, the Uber people kept sending me cars that weren't big enough for the chair. Sebastian, get me a drink, would you? Why on earth are you all standing out here? It's freezing, you'll catch a death.

Margaret looks at the scene before her and notices the tension.

Missed something, have I? Emma, where's that lovely girl of yours?

Erica, Joy corrects her.

They broke up, Seb scoffs, and now she's hitting on my wife.

Seb, that's not-

Ooh, drama, I see, Margaret says, and Joy, are you interested at all?

What?

You heard me, are you interested in the advances of this woman? She gestures to Erica, her black and white wig blowing nefariously in the breeze.

I... this is- what? Joy feels her face redden; this is not how this is supposed to happen.

Oh my god, Seb says, is that what this is about?

I... Seb, I think we need to talk somewhere, just us.

You are *joking*?!

Panic rises inside of Joy as she looks from Erica to Seb, scrambling for words, the right words. Nothing is coming out, nothing is forming in her head, she wants to grab Erica's hand and run and run and run, she can feel her face getting hotter as she stumbles over her words. She is squirming under Seb's gaze, and he knows it. Margaret looks on amused, as if this were a skit they had planned to put on for her entertainment.

She tries to form words, but she can feel her hands getting clammy, the nausea rising, her mouth goes dry and then is suddenly full of saliva. She runs to a nearby plant pot and throws up her last four drinks, and a surprising amount of cheese and pineapple sticks into it. Erica is behind her immediately, stroking her back.

I've told that girl, Margaret says loudly, take a test.

She laughs to herself, as if Joy's potential pregnancy were a joke, and wheels her way back into the bar, once again batting at strangers who didn't immediately move for her.

Joy squeezes her eyes tightly, had they both heard that? Did they understand the meaning of it? She doesn't want to look up from the plant pot, but suddenly feels the absence of Erica's warm, comforting hand on her back.

Test? Seb asks.

She turns from the plant pot and sits next to it on the ground, tired of everything.

What test, Joy? Erica's voice sounds wobbly, Joy cannot look at her.

Are you… are you pregnant? Seb asks again, quietly.

Joy is silent for a moment and then,

I don't know.

Within seconds, he has hoisted Joy off the floor, her hand tightly grasped in his as he pulls her through the beer garden and into the bar, batting off the questions of Val as they make their exit. Joy tries to look back for Erica, but can't see her. She lets herself be pulled away, once again, from what she wants.

39

10:39PM. OCTOBER 31ST 2019 / LIVERPOOL

Val eventually finds Erica alone at a bar down the street, she had tried to follow after Joy, but lost them, landing instead in a nearby pub. She couldn't have faced going home, not without Joy.

The pair of them sit at a table in the corner, both nursing different brightly coloured sickly-sweet cocktails. No words have needed to be exchanged, just the understanding that Val gets it, and is here if Erica needs to let anything out. So far, they have just sipped at their tepid drinks, dejectedly picking at a bowl of nuts of indeterminate age that sits in-between them.

You love her, yeh?

Obviously.

She loves you too.

I know.

Even at uni, fucking hell, you wouldn't believe it. She would mope around like she was in some sort of breakup movie, compared everyone to you, brought you up in every conversation she could. It was maddening.

Sounds it.

And then obviously I moved here and still knew all that, but didn't want to say anything. She was married and lived so far away and, eurgh, bla bla bla.

Erica nods into her drink.

But it's obvious, Val continues, I think it's obvious. You guys fit each other.

She's pregnant, V, I can't believe it.

No, she *might* be, there's a massive difference.

Silence resumes again and they sip at their drinks some more. Val takes a deep breath and clears her throat.

I've been having an affair with Seb, she says, for years.

Erica looks up from her drink then, takes in her friend in front of her. Beautiful, undeniably, but broken, quietly. Erica has watched her battle herself over and over again the last few years, watched her lose weight, watched her drink too much, watched her overcompensate, watched her hurt herself, watched her laugh. Now, she looks at her, with her Halloween makeup a little smeared, cat ears in disarray, finally trying to make the right decisions.

He doesn't deserve either of you, Erica says.

40

11:16PM. OCTOBER 31ST 2019 / LIVERPOOL

Erica makes the train with seconds to spare, sliding expertly through the slowly closing doors of the Merseyrail carriage, the conductor on the platform trying to kill her with his eyes as she does so. She smiles an apology. If he knew the situation, he'd understand, surely.

She watches as the view turns from city to suburbs and lets the rhythm of the train calm her breathing. She had bolted it down to Liverpool Central Station after Val's confession, trying to formulate a plan in her head as she dodged drunken students dressed as Where's Wally.

She watches as Litherland becomes Waterloo, not long to go now. Butterflies run rampant in her stomach, but she needs to do this. Needs to show up for Joy, needs to let her know that she's going to be here, baby or no baby, and that they should be together regardless. She is going to tell her that she loves her, only her, always her, and that it will stay that way.

Erica imagines Joy opening the front door and flinging herself into her arms, as Seb and his witch of a mother look on in disgust, but they won't care, because they are in love and are going to be those Totally Cool Lesbian Mothers who let their kid dye their hair and teach them how to build tree houses. Erica needs to learn how to build tree houses. And she will hold Joy so tightly and wrangle the dog and take them both home with her as 'Bad Reputation' by Joan Jett plays from somewhere in the background.

And they will live happily ever after.

41

11:47PM. OCTOBER 31ST 2019 / LIVERPOOL

Nobody is home, the car is gone, the dog is not barking, the lights are off. They have gone back to London.

42

NOVEMBER 2019 / LONDON

Joy rinses her hands under the cold-water tap, absentmindedly rubs soap into them. It smells like roses, a gift that she remembers getting from Margaret for Christmas a year or so ago, she is very fond of gifting overpriced soaps. The smell makes her feel sick.

She turns the tap off and sits on the toilet with the seat down, wipes her hands on one of their fluffy towels, another gift from his mother. Joy thinks back to her flat in uni when she, Val and Meg had one towel each. On laundry day they would all hang off different doors in their mildly damp flat, each displaying a different member of The Powerpuff Girls. Seb said they were childish. Joy threw her beloved Buttercup towel out before she moved in with him, these fancy fluffy ones taking its place. She finds a loose thread in the towel and pulls at it, wraps it tightly around the tip of her finger and watches the skin turn from pink to red to purple before letting it go loose. She risks a glance towards the plastic stick that is resting on the side of the bathtub, quickly averts her eyes again. It isn't ready yet, neither is she.

She pulls the towel into her lap, scrunches it between her fists, considers screaming into it. Would he be able to hear her from the other side of the door? She knows he is out there, waiting, like a creepy doll in a horror film. He refused to let her do this alone, but she drew the line at the bathroom door. It's awkward enough trying to not piss all over your hands without a man standing over you and asking if you're sure you're doing it right. She hasn't been sick since Halloween, but Seb is convinced. Nice one, Margaret.

Perfect timing, is what Seb had said on the journey back to London, *just what we need*, he insisted without irony. *We've been drifting apart*, he continued, *and this is just what we need to bring us back together*, he finished, as he pushed a green tea towards her. She had sipped at it, choked down the hatred that she felt for him in that moment. It somehow hadn't occurred to him to address what he had seen in the beer garden, or the half admission that she had made about her feelings towards Erica, not now that there was a maybe-baby inside of her. As if popping a kid out would solve any and all of their issues. As if that was some almighty answer that they had both somehow missed in order to save their unhappy marriage.

Her phone buzzes, an alarm to let her know that three minutes have passed, that she can look at it now. She can't just yet.

She flicks off the alarm and is confronted by Erica's name. It floods her screen, has done since the party. She cannot bring herself to reply, not until she knows if there's a thing living inside of her or not. When they first got back to London, Erica's messages were worried, sad, she had tried to find her, found an empty house, was Joy coming back? Had she taken a test? Was she okay? I got a new smiley face lighter, wanna see a pic? After that, the messages started getting an edge to them. Had Joy just run away from her problems like always? Was Erica just a thing that she thought she could play with? Why could she never keep up her end of the bargain? And then, after another day or two, wounding. How could she break her heart like this all over again?

That last message Joy almost replied to. She couldn't explain. Didn't have the words. She is being cowardly, and she knows it, but what is there to say? Joy has wanted nothing more than to hear her voice the past few days, today, wants to hear her tell her that everything will be okay, but she can't do it. This is her mess, hers. She can't have such selfish expectations of the woman that she loves.

She thinks about Erica back at her flat in Liverpool, heartbroken because of her actions, again. Everything in her body wants to run to her. She refuses to let herself think about what could be if this little plastic stick covered in piss gives her the news that she so desperately wants, no news.

Joy? It's been a while now.

His voice is full of hopeful concern, and she despises him for it. He has been tiptoeing around her since their return to London, treating her as if she is made of glass. She finds it infuriating.

Just another minute, she shouts through the door, chewing on the side of her fingernail.

Deep breath, deep breath, deep breath.

She throws the towel to the ground and stands up, picks up the stick from the side of the bath with a sweaty hand, looks to see which heartbreak she must endure.

Seb? It's ready.

*

Negative.

Joy and Seb sit on the edge of their bed together, looking at the plastic stick that holds no future in its window. Seb looks crushed. Joy is trying to hide her elatedness, relief seeping out of every pore. Despite recent events, it still hurts her to see him sad, she doesn't want him to be unhappy. But she can't do this anymore.

Seb, I think we need to talk, she starts as she tosses the stick into the bin across the room, pretends that she isn't proud of herself when it goes in first time.

Yes, we do, he nods.

She breathes a sigh of relief and takes a breath to speak, when he cuts over her.

I've been sleeping with Val. For some time now.

Joy stares at the expensive carpet. She remembers when they had it fitted, the invoice that came through a few days later for more money than she'd spend on an entire house, let alone the floor of it. They had tried so hard not to stain it at first, all drinks carefully held, no muddy dog paws allowed. As she digests the words that Seb just put into the space between them, she looks for a faint yellow stain from when Bernie was a puppy and she'd fed him cheese, he threw it up in the corner. She cleaned it up as best she could and hid it by covering it with the bin.

I know, I think.

I'm sorry.

No, you're not.

Silence for a moment.

This is over, isn't it?

I think it has been for a while.

Seb nods then, reaches for her hand on the duvet between them. She lets him take it, thinks back to a time when this action would have sent sparks flying through her, but now, nothing.

What do we do now? He asks.

Joy knows exactly what she needs to do.

43

2019 / LIVERPOOL

Erica checks her phone for what feels like the billionth time that day. Still nothing. It had gotten to the point of silence wherein she'd called up O2 to make sure that her phone was working as it should.

It was.

She moves out to her balcony, a thick blanket wrapped around her, bottle of wine in her hand. For a moment, she briefly considers throwing her phone over the edge, freeing herself of its vice grip on her, of Joy's grip on her, but then she'd have to go and get takeaway in person and that sounds like an extra circle of hell that she doesn't need right now.

She sits down in her hanging egg chair, positioned perfectly on the first week she moved in so that she could see the cathedral, and also into some of her neighbours' windows for when she was feeling nosey. She hasn't seen much of note yet, other than the middle-aged couple over the way have a very loud fight, and then very loud makeup sex, which she had quickly retreated back inside her flat for. She lets the breeze sway the chair, lets it comfort her, lets the wine go warm in her hands. She feels around in her pockets for her cigarettes, nothing but the new smiley face lighter is in there.

Shit.

She has already been down to the off license next to her building twice today, which is apparently frequent enough for the guy who works there to comment on her alcohol consumption. She can't face going back down for cigarettes. She lets out a groan and pulls the new lighter out of her pocket, holds it in her hand.

She thought it would be a sweet gesture, to replace the old one, for them to have this shared moment of letting go of something from the past and replacing it with a shiny new thing.

She feels stupid now.

She gets out her phone again and hits Val's number. She answers quickly, she always does.

Speak?

Hello to you too.

Ha, hey babes, you doing alright?

Not great. Still silence from Joy. Have you heard anything?

Not a thing, fucking seagulls, sorry, walking through L1, honestly why do tourists insist on eating Greggs in the middle of the street? Do they like being assaulted by giant birds?

Erica says nothing.

Look, babes, I haven't heard anything either. I'm sure if she was pregnant, I'd have heard about it.

Unless he told her about you.

Erica hears a big sigh down the phone.

I did what I did, it's down to me to deal with what comes after it.

Wow, that's surprisingly grown up.

Yes, I've done a lot of maturing since having an affair.

God, I should hate you.

Probably.

I don't, though.

I know. Look, I'm on my way to Jack's, I gotta go, but stop moping, please. It was painful enough to deal with Joy after your last breakup, don't make me deal with you during this one.

Such a good friend.

Love you babes, it's gonna be fine, promise.

Kay. Have fun with your bar man.

Always.

She hangs up then, leaving silence pressed to Erica's ear. Val is right, she needs to sort herself out. What, is she supposed to just sit around rotting in her flat until somebody new comes along? Well, nobody is ever going to come along if she never brushes her hair and smells like an ashtray.

That's it, she thinks, she can quit smoking. That can be the first step into her new life without Joy. Get rid of the nasty habit, start fresh, start healthy.

Yes, perfect, she feels better already, she thinks as she pulls her coat on and locks the front door to the flat.

She will buy one more pack from the shop downstairs, and then once that one is gone, quit. Or maybe like one more pack after that.

The lift arrives at her floor, and she steps in, surveys herself in the full-length mirrors. She hates this lift, mostly because of the lighting. There is nothing quite as sobering as returning from a night out at three in the morning to be confronted with the sight of yourself with smudged makeup, hair in disarray and clutching onto a sweaty McDonalds bag like it is the secret to eternal life. She gets out at the ground floor, resolute in never thinking about Joy again, and getting on with her life. She opens the front door to the building.

There she is.

Erica rubs her eyes, just to be sure. But yes, she is right. Leaning against the wall of her building, a small suitcase and Bernie at her side, is Joy. She holds a pack of cigarettes in her hand, smiles conspiratorially at Erica, and holds one out to her, puts another between her own lips.

Erica, a teenager again, mentally slaps herself in the face, and moves towards her, takes the cigarette from her hand.

Do you have a lighter? Joy asks.

Yes, Erica says, retrieving the new neon smiley face lighter from her pocket, lifting the flame to both of their mouths. Joy takes the lighter from her.

Erica leans against the wall next to her, their hands touching in the space between them.

She watches Joy's smiling side profile, as she pockets the neon smiley face, and blows smoke into the crisp November air.

ACKNOWLEDGEMENTS

First of all, thank you to the wonderful team at Northodox for believing in this book, for the amazing cover art, and for helping make the book the best it could be. Thank you to everyone that I did my MA in Writing with, this wouldn't be what it is without you guys. A special thanks to James, most of this book was written in your living room, and I am eternally grateful for the never-ending advice and after-writing pints.

Thank you to my family and my beautiful friends (you know who you are), for lending me your unwavering support by listening to me crack on about this book, reading early drafts, and pushing me to carry on when I hit roadblocks. A big thank you to Cam for being my ideal reader, always, and to Olly, just for being Olly, I love you all endlessly.

A big fat thank you to the wonderfully weird humans that I work with, who make my silly and brilliant job of tattooing all the more silly and brilliant. Oh, and apologies to Nick; I'm sorry that this book isn't full of dragons and magic pebbles, I hate to disappoint.

Thank you to Simon, for your support, your love, and for letting me create a room in the house where I can shut the world out (including the dogs) and crack on with writing.

And finally, thank you to everyone who picked up this book and read it, or even just kept it in and endless TBR pile, I appreciate it more than you know.

Milton Keynes UK
Ingram Content Group UK Ltd.
UKHW042152130224
437787UK00002B/4